Brace for Impact

As Craig and Toby struggle to keep their faltering marriage alive, the climate crisis intrudes, part of a threesome in their relationship.

Craig wants to take drastic action but Toby just wants to live his life as best he can before climate breakdown escalates.

“You fight for your life by any means necessary,” Craig insists. “If someone breaks into your house, you pull out a baseball bat or a gun. When there’s a mass shooting, you run, you hide, or you fight back.”

But when it involves global warming? And fossil fuel industries buying politicians who protect carbon emissions at the cost of human lives?

Craig wonders if a letter to the editor is enough. If blocking traffic at a rally once or twice a year is effective.

Toby threatens to leave him if does anything stupid. And to report him to the authorities.

But Craig feels he’ll need to commit violence one way or another, either by condoning the status quo or by doing whatever he can to fight those who keep destabilizing the climate. So he joins a group of eco activists whose efforts are far more extreme than even he had expected.

Will Craig survive the violent police crackdown on protesters?

Will his relationship with Toby survive the additional stress of betrayal?

And will either of them survive the new wildfire that's just started at the edge of town?

Praise for Johnny Townsend

In *Zombies for Jesus*, "Townsend isn't writing satire, but deeply emotional and revealing portraits of people who are, with a few exceptions, quite lovable."

Kel Munger, *Sacramento News and Review*

In *Sex among the Saints,* "Townsend writes with a deadpan wit and a supple, realistic prose that's full of psychological empathy….he takes his protagonists' moral struggles seriously and invests them with real emotional resonance."

Kirkus Reviews

Inferno in the French Quarter: The UpStairs Lounge Fire is "a gripping account of all the horrors that transpired that night, as well as a respectful remembrance of the victims."

Terry Firma, Patheos

"Johnny Townsend's 'Partying with St. Roch' [in the anthology *Latter-Gay Saints*] tells a beautiful, haunting tale."

Kent Brintnall, Out in Print: Queer Book Reviews

Selling the City of Enoch is "sharply intelligent...pleasingly complex...The stories are full of...doubters, but there's no vindictiveness in these pages; the characters continuously poke holes in Mormonism's more extravagant absurdities, but they take very little pleasure in doing so....Many of Townsend's stories...have a provocative edge to them, but this [book] displays a great deal of insight as well...a playful, biting and surprisingly warm collection."

Kirkus Reviews

Gayrabian Nights is "an allegorical tour de force...a hard-core emotional punch."

Gay. Guy. Reading and Friends

The Washing of Brains has "A lovely writing style, and each story [is] full of unique, engaging characters....immensely entertaining."

Rainbow Awards

In *Dead Mankind Walking*, "Townsend writes in an energetic prose that balances crankiness and humor....A rambunctious volume of short, well-crafted essays..."

Kirkus Reviews

Brace for Impact

Johnny Townsend

Print ISBN: 978-1-961525-26-9
Ebook ISBN: 978-1-961525-27-6

Printed on acid-free paper.

2024

Second Edition

(Original title: Please Evacuate Again)

Cover design by Bravo Book Covers

Contents

Phone a Friend

"Hi Maggie," I said when she answered. "How're you doing? Enjoying your garden?" We were both on video, so I could see she was puttering behind her house.

"All right, Craig. What did you and Toby fight about this time?"

I chuckled despite myself. She knew me too well. "Tell me about your flowers first."

"You won't hear a single word I'm saying until you've gotten things off your chest," she insisted. "Spill."

Maggie and I had earned our biology degrees in Boulder decades ago. I'd hoped to do grand things but hadn't even managed to get into a doctorate program, moving instead to Seattle to start a new "career" as a bartender on Capitol Hill. Maggie had gone on to teach at a public university in Texas, finally retiring at the end of the spring semester earlier this year.

Her medium-brown hair showed several gray strands, but she still looked to be in her early fifties, not mid-sixties. My own hair was salt and pepper, more salt these days than pepper. It used to be wavy, but I was so tired of bed hair that I kept it clipped short now. My moustache was almost pure white.

In my head, I was Sam Elliott. In the mirror I was Wilford Brimley.

The first thing Maggie had done once free of tenure was move to a small town in northern California, certainly a more tempting visit for Toby and me.

"Even small-town small mindedness in California is better than college town small mindedness in Texas," she'd explained at the time. Her husband Gary, a native Texan, was taking a bit longer to make the decision to follow, but with another heatwave followed by another tropical storm making his loneliness lonelier, he was wrapping things up as quickly as possible.

"Craig? Are you there?" Maggie whistled, bringing me back into focus. "You going to tell me what the latest battle with Toby is?"

I chuckled again. "You know what he's like," I said. He'd done nothing new or especially offensive. My tolerance of his behavior was simply dwindling. That often felt like more of a failure on my part than his.

"He's still checking up on you?" Maggie asked.

"We're in a goddamn open relationship," I repeated for the hundredth time. "But if I take too long at the grocery, he gets suspicious. I have no control over the buses. And what difference does it make if I have sex with someone else, anyway? He does it, too. And we haven't had sex with each other in almost a year and a half."

Just rehashing the same story again and again. Maggie was good to put up with it. The stories she repeated were always about her good students, not even the annoying ones.

"Craig," she said, "does it really count as an open relationship if *you two* don't have sex?"

I hated the question, but she'd asked it before and I'd known she'd ask it again today.

Wasn't that why I'd called?

Even in my twenties, I'd enjoyed sex with older men and never had the expectation that men in their sixties faced this level of frustration. Toby was seventy, for goodness' sake, and I still found him hot.

I was only sixty-two. Why couldn't he still want me?

Maggie and I talked several more minutes, discussing the pros and cons of staying married, breaking up, or staying partners but living separately. Nothing about the options had changed in the past few years. None of the options felt right.

But were there really any others?

"Do you remember how you felt when you first met Toby?" Maggie asked. She posed the question whenever it was time to stop talking about my frustrations, a polite way to say, "Enough."

And it worked, making me smile. I'd seen Toby one night eating peanuts at the bar where I worked. He chewed like a goat, which is probably why he'd grown a goatee. He was adorable.

Even now, all these years later, I still reacted the same way when I looked at him. That had to be a good sign, right?

"Thanks, Maggie," I said. "Now let's get to your flowers. They're starting to look neglected from my blabbing so long."

She shrugged with a light laugh, both of us eager, I figured, to change the subject. Positive people usually only hung out with other positive people, afraid of energy drain. I supposed I was a mix of both positive and negative, which was why she put up with me. I gave people compliments, an easy way to introduce at least a spark of light into the world. I mowed my neighbor Christopher's lawn because he loathed doing it himself. And I saved coupons for my regulars at the drugstore.

I could probably stand to develop my positive side a bit more.

"Marigolds are always cheerful," Maggie said. "But with the dry weather, I'm out here every day watering." She glanced upward. "Looks like it's getting cloudy, though. Maybe we'll get a little rain."

Maggie had settled into her new home too late to plant vegetables this year, focusing instead on flowers. She wanted beauty and peace after so many years of stress. The chair of her department had grown up in Uvalde, and the terrible shooting there had colored Maggie's last year of classes.

So we talked for another ten minutes about flowers. California poppies could hardly be beat for collective beauty and Maggie hoped to plant an entire acre with them next year. She hoped to add meadow lupines at some point, too. Maybe some baby blue eyes.

She and Gary had chosen not to have children, investing their energy into helping other people's children. He taught chemistry and had retired three years ago.

Maggie had been sitting cross-legged on the ground as we chatted and now stared into the sky. She frowned.

"What?" I squinted at the tiny screen.

She stood and pointed her phone upward. I couldn't quite make out what I was seeing. "Is that smoke?"

"There were no wildfires yesterday," she said, "but I haven't listened to the news today. I needed a break after all the indictments. And that latest killing over a Pride flag."

Maggie was a fierce ally and flew her rainbow flag even in a rural red county.

She started back for her house and then stopped, her face tense.

"What?" I asked again.

"I hear it now," she said. Maggie turned the corner and let me glimpse what she was seeing. Maybe half a mile away, trees were burning.

So was a house.

As we watched, the flames burst forward at an impossible speed. Even a minute ago, they must have been nowhere near that home. Now they overtook a car racing away from it.

We watched as the car veered wildly and crashed into a ditch.

"Maggie! Get out of there!"

Suddenly, the images on my phone revealed nothing but blurred, frantic jerks. It hurt to look but of course I kept looking. All I could hear at first was panting. But soon I heard a roar of crackling, too.

Silence then as Maggie entered her home, but still no clear images as she rummaged about for car keys. Then she was back outside where the shaking images took on an orange glow.

I saw Maggie's blue Sonata for a moment before she turned the phone back toward the fire. The flames were much closer now. Another home was burning. A man perhaps forty and a young girl maybe eight were running at full speed away from the building. The car parked beside the house was already ablaze.

"Carrie and Dave!" Maggie breathed.

"Drive!" I shouted.

I remembered a scene from a TV movie about a plane crash in the Potomac as an elderly woman watched a survivor about to drown during a live newsbreak. "Swim, Priscilla, swim!" she'd shouted at the television, willing her energy to reach her granddaughter.

More blurry images followed, and I heard the car engine come to life. The phone now rested in a holder on the dashboard, and I watched Maggie concentrate as she pulled away from her new home.

She screeched to a halt and looked off to her right.

"Oh my god!" This time she screamed the words, shock and horror in her eyes. "They're on fire!"

"Drive, Maggie, drive!"

I could hear her gunning the engine and see her staring straight ahead. Her face jiggled a little as the car bounced over bumps in the road. Seconds passed. Then a couple more. It felt like an eternity.

I saw Maggie glance into the rearview mirror and watched as her expression slackened. There was no fear. No visible emotion at all.

"Tell Gary I love him," she said.

I should have turned away.

But I watched Maggie as the flames enveloped her. And heard her screaming in agony for fifteen soul-crushing seconds before the phone finally cut out.

Haze

I moved slowly the next few days, performing by rote, barely awake, despite being accused of being woke by my supervisor at the drugstore in Mount Baker.

A neo-Nazi was caught shooting at a power substation near Portland moments before he might have knocked out the electric grid.

Scientists recorded the hottest June ever.

Phoenix endured more than thirty days in a row of 110-degree or higher temperatures. Even the saguaros began dying.

2500-year-old baobab trees in South Africa were dying.

Climatologists measured the hottest ocean temperature ever recorded, over a hundred degrees—hot tub temperature—off the coast of Florida.

Portugal and Spain and Algeria and Sicily suffered catastrophic wildfires. Greece and Morocco and Canada, too.

And California.

A ship carrying 3000 cars off the coast of Norway sank after an explosion. Authorities couldn't determine if the ship was attacked by drones from Russia trying to expand its war against Ukraine. Or if a defective car battery had ignited. Or if the fire had been caused by something else altogether.

Holding Hands

Toby held my hand as we sat on the sofa, our thighs touching. *Heartstopper* played on Netflix. I'd resisted the show, not interested in stories about teens coming out, but I'd heard that despite being a bit sappy it was genuinely sweet, not saccharine, and I'd succumbed.

Maggie had sworn it was worth my time.

Toby had been nothing but solicitous in the days after the fire. He even drove to a produce stand on Beacon Hill to purchase some boiled peanuts, a rarity in the Pacific Northwest. We'd tried them on a trip to New Orleans once and I'd loved them. Toby had been less impressed. But he bought a pound of them for me two days ago.

And today, he bought me a loaf of keto bread so I could have toast for the first time in years.

He was nodding off now, but I knew better than to wake him. I watched as rugby player Nick struggled with the realization he was gay or bi and that his life was going to change whether he was ready for it or not.

The show was short. After two episodes, I carefully reached for the remote in my lap and turned Netflix off. A hot column of sunshine beaming through the window beside our front door had made the image on almost half the TV screen impossible to see in any event. I wanted to put curtains on the two little windows on each side of the door, but Toby wouldn't have it. Sometimes I put a manila folder up there. He hated that even more.

Toby stirred.

"Did we like it?" he murmured.

"You swooned," I said. "Don't you remember? Why do you think you fell unconscious?"

He stood slowly and stretched. "Let me get some cereal and we'll watch something else."

Toby headed for the kitchen, limping slightly from arthritis in his right knee, barely noticeable except when he first woke up. I heard him pull down a Rubbermaid container of oat rings, pour the cereal into a bowl, and cover them with oat milk.

Oats were good for healthy hearts.

Too many carbs for me, of course. I'd been on semaglutide for six months and had lost fifty pounds, no longer on insulin, my A1C down to 5.4. But I still watched my carbs.

"What are you in the mood for?" I asked. We agreed on most shows, though I was more likely to watch something "serious" like *A Small Light* or *The Handmaid's Tale*. Toby could barely tolerate *Resident Alien*, growing anxious when the doctor plotted to kill the kid who realized he wasn't human.

A comedy, it made Toby nervous. He walked out of the room when things grew too tense. I wanted to watch a new show about gay leathermen. Toby used to like seeing me in my harness. I'd given it away years ago after it no longer fit. If I'd kept it, I could probably fit into it again now.

Perhaps I should start saving for a new one.

It might soon be too hot to sustain a leather community, I realized. I used to sweat in my chaps even in winter.

"How about *Unbreakable Kimmy Schmidt*?" he asked.

I pulled it up on the screen.

"Thanks, Craig." He leaned over to kiss me before digging into his cereal.

It was difficult not to be acutely aware of my own mortality after Maggie's death, and sometimes, I wondered if I was frittering away my remaining hours watching frivolous shows I didn't care about.

But this was our "together" time. We had to do *something* as a couple, after all, and there weren't many options left. Toby's eyesight wasn't great, even after his cataract surgery, so dragon puzzles were a thing of the past. Scrabble had grown too frustrating because Toby couldn't spell and felt affronted if I challenged a word. I'd finally stopped challenging, which meant he almost always won, and that was fine. We were having fun.

We used to play it all the time.

Despite his own difficulty seeing details clearly, Toby frequently greeted me at the door with, "Notice anything different?" He'd asked it again today.

"Um, you dusted," I ventured. I could hardly say more of his hair had turned white. It was practically all white now, a color that looked great on him but which made him feel old. He would only trim his hair while wet because the snipped off parts then looked gray in the sink, and gray apparently didn't make him feel as old as white.

"I did that days ago."

"Uh, you moved the yellow vase."

"Nope." He sighed. "You know, if you loved me, you'd notice the things I do around here."

He wouldn't tell me what he'd done, though, demanding I figure it out on my own and then let him know when I had.

I looked about the room for several more seconds and gave up.

Toby and I were barely ten minutes into the next episode of *Kimmy Schmidt* when I heard his phone ding. He reached over to the end table and checked the text, smiling before beginning to text something back.

I put the show on Pause.

Toby hit Send and set the phone down, so I hit Play.

Twenty seconds later, his phone pinged again, and he picked it up. I hit Pause once more and leaned back with my eyes closed while Toby texted with one of his friends for the next five or six minutes.

When he finally set his phone aside at what appeared to be the end of the conversation, he looked at me quizzically. "You didn't have to Pause it."

It was either that or have him ask me twenty questions to catch up. There was no point in explaining my reasons, of course. I just smiled and hit Play.

Toby grabbed my hand, put it on his thigh, and we continued watching.

"He's kind of cute," Toby said, indicating one of the actors, a man about forty. "Nice ass."

"Yep," I agreed. "But not as nice as yours."

"Mine's old and flabby."

"Your ass isn't flabby."

"Just old?"

"Of course it's old. Seventy years old, like the rest of your body. But still beautiful." I wasn't trying to flatter him. Toby's smooth ass was one of his best features. Hairless and firm, it was still kissable, lickable, and fuckable.

What more could anyone ask of their ass?

"Hmmph. Thanks."

"I wish you'd let me see it more often."

We slept separately because of my sleep apnea. I spent the night sitting up on the sofa while he had the bedroom to himself. I might catch a glimpse of him taking his clothes off just before he climbed into bed, but that was about the extent of it. I could hear him beating off sometimes after lights out, but he never let me watch anymore.

Toby's brows furrowed as he concentrated on the screen before us, but we so rarely came even this close to a real conversation that I felt I needed to take advantage of the opportunity. I hit Pause.

"I weigh 190 now," I said. "Do you think you'll ever feel attracted to me again?"

"I never said I didn't find you attractive."

"You just stopped having sex with me."

"It's not like you ask very often."

Toby had turned me down six of the last eight times I'd asked. "And you haven't asked *me* in ten years."

Toby's eyes darted from the paused TV screen over to the remote and back to the screen again.

Gray eyes whose color I didn't notice until our fifth or sixth date. He had a point about my failure to notice detail.

"I've always found you attractive," Toby insisted. "I just lost interest because some of your body parts weren't working."

I felt momentarily confused. I'd naturally assumed my weight was the issue. Was Toby saying he was turned off when my fingertips grew slightly crooked because of my own arthritis? Because I couldn't shoot as far? Was it because my knees popped sometimes? I mentally surveyed my body.

"You stopped having sex with me because I got leg cramps when we were fucking?"

He turned his head, and our eyes met.

Oh.

Toby had stopped having sex with me because two times in a row, I'd had a difficult time staying hard.

He took ED pills himself. And he couldn't simply suggest I do the same? In fact, I *had* asked my doctor for a prescription shortly after that, and Toby knew it.

"Jesus Christ. We're talking about sex and you can't even say 'erection' or 'hard'?" We weren't children, after all. We didn't need to say "your wee wee."

"See? I knew you'd get upset. That's why I never said anything."

Toby carried his bowl to the kitchen. I heard him put it in the sink. Without rinsing. And then he walked to his office at the back of the house.

I turned off the television and headed to my office at the front of the house. I logged onto FB and scrolled through pictures of my friends' cats and dogs and freshly knitted scarves.

And for some sadistic reason, the algorithms decided I wanted to see photos of exquisitely beautiful, sugary cakes posted by complete strangers.

Why hadn't Toby told me what he was thinking? It had been *years*. We were about to celebrate our twenty-first anniversary. Intellectually, I understood that sex wasn't always as high a priority as couples aged, but this?

I continued looking to FB for relief.

Roger, a deaf friend of mine in San Francisco, posted a cartoon showing a father and son stepping out of a car in front of a suburban home with two cooked fish on a pole. They were greeted by a woman at the door. The father announced, "Every fish in the lake was cooked by the time we got there."

I noticed now that his hair looked singed. There was a thick plume of smoke in the corner of the cartoon, in the distance as a remote mountain burned.

Maggie had wanted to spend a week in the Amazon jungle before too much of it was cut down. She'd hoped to go in January or February if she could persuade Gary.

Toby got miffed if I took the ferry to Vashon without him, but whenever I asked if he wanted to go, he'd say it was too cold on the Sound.

Why couldn't he ask me to wear a cock ring? Maybe he'd been afraid of hurting my feelings, that I was too fragile to handle the news.

When my twin sister had developed non-Hodgkin lymphoma at the age of sixteen, my parents asked the doctor not to tell her the diagnosis. They started Carol on chemotherapy without even asking her.

She at least finally learned the truth before she died.

I had a right to know why I was in a celibate marriage.

I switched to YouTube and listened to Claude Barzotti for a while. I never grew tired of "Le Rital."

Tonight, it wasn't enough.

I sat at my desk and stared at the bookshelves above my monitor. The books and DVDs were my only connection to the outside world. *Roommate* by Sarina Bowen, *The Rules* by Jamie Fessenden, *Now I'm Here* by Jim Provenzano.

And my favorite TV series.

I still loved Lucy.

But these other lives no longer seemed to offer escape. They were bars keeping me confined inside this house, away from real life.

Toby and I had agreed on an open relationship from the start, my first, since my previous two long-term relationships had been monogamous…and suffocating. But I'd never done more than keep an eye open for opportunities once or twice a year. A bus driver here, a bank teller there, even one of the men who came to pick up yard waste each week. I'd quit working at the bar less than a year after we moved in together.

But my cruising had never been methodical. I'd invested most of my sexual energy into complimenting Toby—in complete honesty—on his ass, admiring the slight crook of his nose that made my dick twitch if I looked too long, fantasizing the last several months about the day he'd be interested in me again.

I even tripped him once when he leaned over to kiss me goodnight and pulled him onto my lap, giving him a back rub for five minutes while making my dick pulse as strongly as I could to make sure he felt it against his ass, even through two pairs of underwear.

But now…

I searched "gay hook up sites" and was surprised at the variety that popped up. I liked leather but wasn't into S&M. I liked barebacking, but after browsing for only two minutes saw over ten photographic offers of "cum dumps."

I moved on.

Men in Uniform looked too intimidating. Twinks Galore did little for me. Silver Daddies? Maybe. Sexy Grandpas?

Old Guys with Pot Bellies. Was that even a real thing? There was so much satire these days. But I'd sucked off the pot-bellied proprietor of an antique shop on Capitol Hill once and thoroughly enjoyed the experience, so the name of the website wasn't a deal breaker.

I selected two hook up sites, wrote a different profile for each, and uploaded a different face pic for each. A bit risky to show my face, what with the reality of stalkers, but my five and a half inch dick wasn't going to provide enough bait to get me further than five and a half inches.

I took a couple of nude selfies with my phone, shrugged at the results, and added them to my "gallery." Then I hit Submit.

Hundreds of local men were on both sites. I only needed two or three fuck buddies to feel alive again. But while waiting for the requests to start trickling in, I scrolled through the other profiles.

"No boring back and forth!" one man demanded. "I'm here to fuck!"

Me, too, but now you seem too rude to approach.

"I can't get hard but I can still suck."

Hmm. Perhaps I could understand Toby's perspective better now, as I didn't find such an offer overly tempting, either.

There was a tap on my office door. “Good night, Craig.”

I opened the door and gave Toby a peck. “Night, sweetie.”

“Love you.”

“I love you, too.” I had to consciously keep myself from sighing. I expected we were both telling the truth. I simply wasn’t sure anymore if love was enough.

Toby went into his bedroom and shut the door. I sat again at my desk and listened through the wall as he beat off, feeling lonelier than ever.

Sixty-two years wasn’t a bad run. Maybe I didn’t need to stick around very much longer. If I wasn’t enjoying life and I wasn’t doing anything to make the world a better place…

I tried to beat off to the pics on Nipple Man’s profile but couldn’t reach climax, too distracted by the name of this new superhero to figure out what I needed to do to save myself.

Connecting Flight

"Hey, Craig." Kaymeena waved from the driveway next door, adjusting the position of her yard waste bin near the curb. She and her husband Christopher had moved in maybe ten years earlier. Toby chatted with them more than I did, let me know when their oldest daughter went off to study in Argentina, when their youngest left for school in Chicago.

I tried to be polite but always felt I was intruding. I instinctively assumed neighbors felt trapped by their own politeness if I started chatting outside. They probably had chores to do and didn't want to be bothered.

"Hi, Kaymeena. How're you guys?"

Christopher usually looked the other way if I saw him, pretending not to see me, perhaps embarrassed about the lawn mowing.

"Loving this hot weather." She laughed lightly. "I know *you* hate it. Toby tells me you insist on keeping the house at 55 in the winter."

"Once it hits 60, I need at least the fan on."

Kaymeena hugged herself involuntarily. She wore a sweater that draped almost to her knees. The temperature had to be over 70 even this early in the morning. Her braids hung low past her shoulders like an additional blanket. "I can recommend a therapist," she teased.

"I might need two," I told her. People who loved the heat were certainly going to enjoy better mental health in the coming years than fossils like me.

Kaymeena waved goodbye as she headed back inside, and I continued on to Renton Avenue. I'd taken a vacation day without telling Toby and was determined to make a meager attempt at regaining control of my life. I'd had no luck yet meeting anyone online. There was an adult video store with an arcade and theater in White Center, but it took three buses to get there.

I'd found another video store listing down in Des Moines, which was farther away but easier to reach. I caught the 106 to the light rail station and then took the train to the last stop in Angle Lake. After a two-minute wait for the Express A, I was soon on 216th.

From there, it was only a short walk to Lucky Video.

Or so I thought. On the map, the store looked to be less than two blocks from the intersection, but I walked five blocks in each direction without ever finding it. The only indication I was in the right neighborhood was a sign proclaiming, "Designated Prostitution Vehicle Impound Area."

After searching in vain for an hour and fifteen minutes, I headed back to the light rail station. It had to be over 80 degrees now, warm for Seattle. I bought a lottery ticket at a 7-11 and then went ahead and swallowed my dick pill just in case.

I'd taken four fiber capsules with a glass of water for breakfast to fill my stomach and though I felt both tired and hot, I decided to keep walking and try to lose another ounce. I headed north on International Boulevard. It wasn't all that far to the SeaTac Airport light rail station.

And it wasn't as if I had anything better to do.

I'd barely passed Angle Lake Park when I noticed folks ahead lined up along the sidewalks on both sides of the street. As I approached, I realized they were flight attendants for a major airline.

Hundreds and hundreds and hundreds of them. All waving signs.

#1 in Customer Satisfaction. #6 in Pay.

9 Years Without a Contract

Full Pay for All Time Worked

Record Profits, Record Exploitation

Dozens of drivers in both directions honked their support.

"Hi!" A young man about thirty with clipped, dark brown hair waved energetically at me. "You're wearing a red shirt. You a supporter?"

"Um, yes," I said. "Yes, I am." I still had nothing better to do.

The young man handed me a sign that read "Fair Contract for Flight Attendants!" and stepped aside to let me stand next to him.

"I'm Jonah."

Clean shaven, not usually my type, and paler than I preferred, but friendly, which definitely was my type.

"Craig." I moved into the shade of a tree.

He nudged me with his shoulder. "Thanks for showing up."

I experienced a flash of imposter syndrome, but whether planned or not, I was here supporting them now. Drivers continued honking. Flight attendants shouted slogans. Local buses passed, county buses, taxis, ride share drivers. Airport shuttles passed by. UPS drivers honked in support. Truckers driving 18-wheelers honked. Men in pickup trucks honked.

The only people who didn't honk were Amazon drivers.

Jonah noticed me looking at an Amazon van. "They've got video cameras in the vans," he said. "The drivers are afraid to show support."

But almost everyone else did. The energy was infectious. I almost felt good.

No, I *did* feel good. It was all too easy in a constantly negative news cycle to accept that most people didn't give a damn. Over the next hour, though, probably 80% of the hundreds of drivers rushing by honked and waved.

"It's only a honk," Jonah said with a shrug, as if reading my mind after the latest blast from a delivery driver. "It's two seconds of solidarity, but it's not nothing."

"Will it make a difference?"

"It already has."

I couldn't help but raise an eyebrow Spock style.

Jonah laughed. "CEOs are notoriously resistant to public shaming," he said.

"So…"

Jonah waved to the long line of flight attendants. "We're being seen and heard," he said. "We *feel* it. *That* matters to us."

The sun had moved since I'd arrived, so the shade from the tree had moved, and so I moved as well to stay out of the blazing sun. Some of the protesters held umbrellas to create their own shade, but an awful lot of folks seemed unfazed by the heat.

"Feeling hot?" Jonah asked.

"Do you know everything I'm thinking?" I gave him a tiny smile. Flirting was *not* like riding a bike.

Remembering my failure to note the color of Toby's eyes from the start, I looked into Jonah's. Light brown, bordering on golden, not a common color and quite striking. I knew some people judged others by their shoes, but I couldn't care less what shoes someone wore, especially since I preferred a man with no clothes at all.

While watching Jonah hold his protest sign, I did notice that all his fingernails were trimmed identically to reveal a millimeter of white at the tips. A bit anal. Which could be good. I liked anuses.

And he had huge veins on the back of both hands.

I couldn't help but think how useful that might be if he ever needed an IV.

No wonder Toby thought I was weird.

Jonah shrugged. "I know what that smile means," he said. He dug in his pocket and pulled out a card. "Here's my number. We'll be wrapping up here in about half an hour. You have anywhere you need to be?"

I nodded with fake weariness and Jonah scrunched his nose in disappointment.

"Your place," I said then with a smirk.

Jonah grinned. "You *are* a good labor supporter."

"I can support from in front or from behind."

"I think the word you *meant* to use was 'and.'"

Whispers

I'd forgotten how good cum tasted. And how much fun it was to pass back and forth while deep kissing another man.

It was like drinking an ice cold Mexi-Coke on a hot summer day, a feeling of ultimate pleasure.

Up close, I could see that Jonah had a slight ridge on the top of his nose and what appeared to be a single acne scar on his lower left cheek.

"I had a beauty mark removed," he volunteered.

"Sorry for staring."

He shrugged. "Gives me a chance to stare back." Now he grinned. "Hazel eyes and poorly plucked eyebrows."

"Um…"

"It's easier if you just trim them with a beard trimmer. My dad taught me."

No one had taught me—Toby had no such issues—and I felt oddly grateful for the tip. Jonah then presented me with one more, squeezing his dick to force out a last drop of cum. I stretched toward it and licked. Then he kissed me once again.

As we dressed afterward, I finally noticed my surroundings. Framed photos of various airplanes, large and small, lined Jonah's walls. Framed prints of movie posters for *Airport*, *Airplane*, and *Air Force One*. A pewter sculpture of a vintage propeller plane sat on his coffee table.

I realized his loveseat was actually two airline seats, complete with seatbelts and movable armrests. A paper map on one wall was dotted with colored pins presumably marking every location Jonah had traveled to, either for work or pleasure.

And suddenly, all I could think about was the carbon footprint of the airline industry. Jonah seemed like a nice enough guy, and I did support flight attendants. But now I couldn't stop thinking about the ethics of working in such a destructive field.

Which flight was the one that finally pushed California's climate into the danger zone?

"My schedule's crazy," Jonah said as he led me to the door, "but I hope we can do this again."

"Me, too."

Jonah must have caught me staring at one of the posters and frowning. "Almost every job," he said, "supports some corporation that's destroying the planet. Even working from home or living off the grid wouldn't help."

I wasn't sure I liked how easily he could read me.

He leaned over and whispered into my ear the one sex act I was too embarrassed to ask for but which I wanted to try more than any other.

And now I didn't care how he managed to get inside my head.

"Let me know if you guys plan any more rallies."

Jonah gave me another deep kiss before ushering me out the door.

Back home, I added a line to both of my online profiles. "Looking for activist buddies in addition to fuck buddies."

It could hardly reduce the number of invitations I'd been receiving. You couldn't drop lower than zero.

***

I always took my meds with a swig of kombucha, followed by a spoonful of probiotic cottage cheese. A healthy microbiome, Maggie had explained, was essential for weight control, diabetes management, and a strong immune system. There'd been no discussion of gut microbiomes back when I studied biology, but as a professor, Maggie had kept up with the latest scientific discoveries.

Toby hated when I sang "A spoonful of bacteria helps the medicine go down," but it was true, and there were days I couldn't resist at least humming the tune.

I'd be getting no more helpful advice from Maggie.

Toby cooked spicy veggie burgers for dinner with a side of green bean casserole, one of my favorite dishes. I tried to go light on the fried onions and downed a few extra fiber capsules to counteract the carbs. I drank a lime seltzer water while Toby had a cold cup of coffee left over from this morning.

"Notice anything special about the spices?" he asked.

"Um, they're spicy?"

"Hmmph." Toby ate his next few bites in silence. I couldn't understand why he invited unhappiness. Didn't enough come our way all by itself?

"Paying attention to people," he muttered a few moments later, "is sexy." He picked up the remote.

There was no sense mentioning that I'd bought a new Polo shirt, turquoise, now that I could fit into a Large again, and he hadn't said a word. This wasn't a competition I wanted to win.

"Clayton and Ben got their visas today," Toby said as he pulled up something from his list and hit Play. While we tried to eat together whenever possible, the TV was on during every conversation. As I looked at the screen, a documentary about women trying to get into the space program in the early 1960s began playing.

"They're really moving to France?" Clayton and Ben were Toby's friends, not mine, though I knew them superficially.

"They're too afraid to stay," Toby said. The couple lived up in Marysville and had dodged bricks thrown through their front window twice. Someone had spray painted "Predators" on their driveway. Because every LGBTQ person these days was accused of "grooming."

"Do you want to emigrate?" I asked. I spoke some Italian and French, and Toby spoke passable Spanish.

Toby shook his head. "I'm not going to run away like a scared child." He was unable to keep the judgment out of his voice.

Given his general reaction to tense situations, I wanted to suggest he teach Self Awareness 101 at Seattle Central, but there was really no point. Toby was only trying to find a relevant topic to discuss over dinner. We had to talk about something.

"I read an article about the new contract for Metro bus drivers," I said. It was either that or mention the fire at a homeless encampment in north Seattle.

"Yeah?"

"They no longer have recourse if they're discriminated against on the job."

Toby shrugged. "Well, that's the reality today."

I watched an elderly woman on TV describe her feelings the day astronaut training was canceled for the women despite the women uniformly doing better on the sensory deprivation test than any of the men.

"What do you think of the reality in India with something like an 85% increase in heavy rainfall *and* a 50 or 55% increase in drought?" Being a nerd was one thing. It was clear I was becoming obsessed.

Toby didn't answer. His phone pinged, indicating a text, and he put the documentary on Pause while he texted back.

I continued eating, looking up occasionally at the paused screen, archival footage of one of the women being interviewed back in 1962, wearing an elegant dress and high heels to work as a test pilot.

Toby put his phone down and let the documentary continue. "Those stories don't mean anything anymore," he said, and I wasn't sure what he was referring to until he went on. "It's like hearing about another mass shooting. Climate disasters are all background noise now."

"There's a rally next week in front of one of the banks downtown," I said. "To demand they stop giving loans to fossil fuel companies."

"Craig, do we have to talk about this?" He picked up the remote and turned the volume up slightly. I saw the number on the screen rise from 12 to 14. "I don't want to get involved. It's too late to do anything, anyway."

Toby was asleep before the documentary was over. I turned it off and quietly carried the dishes to the kitchen and washed them, wasting way too much water since we didn't have a dishwasher. Then I walked quietly to my office and checked my computer.

I had one response from a man who wanted to be my activist buddy. "Let's fuck first," he said, "and see if we have chemistry. Then if we do, let's activism each other's brains out."

Perhaps he thought I was giving him a line. Perhaps he was giving me one. But what the hell.

I took a deep breath and typed a response. "When can we meet, buddy?"

Rain

Historic flooding devastated parts of Vermont and Italy and Slovenia. Hailstorms damaged crops, cars, and homes across Spain and Germany, across Colorado and Minnesota. Typhoons ravaged the Philippines, Taiwan, and China.

In Texas, public libraries were converted into youth discipline centers. School districts across the country banned books on race, gender, and sexual orientation. Drag shows were banned, even criminalized, in state after state.

In the U.S. southwest, doctors began treating patients who'd tripped and fallen onto the asphalt for third-degree burns. All forty-five beds in one burn unit in Phoenix were filled.

People baked cookies in their cars. Roads buckled or melted.

The governor of Texas banned water breaks for outdoor workers.

A woman in California hosed down a mail carrier who collapsed in her driveway.

UK railway workers went on strike for three days, UK postal workers went on strike for a day and were still in bitter negotiations, university workers in the UK were planning a strike, and the UK's National Health Services were still on strike months after they began.

Signs of Life

"I hope you have a good time at the rally, Craig." Toby kissed me as I headed out the door. He'd made sure I put on sunscreen before leaving.

He'd also helped me improve my sign for the protest. While I'd written down the slogan, "If you break the planet, you don't get your deposit back"—which seemed appropriate enough outside a bank, even if the pun wasn't perfect—he'd suggested I write something on the back, too, so folks could be inspired from either direction.

His suggestion was "Oil companies making record profits don't need loans."

An obvious point I hadn't considered. Just before time to leave, I added underneath that comment, in a different color, the words "or subsidies."

I made sure to hold my sign while on light rail so that other riders could see. It didn't matter if they agreed or not. I wanted them to know there was a climate protest and that someone was making a fuss.

I'd looked up comedies about protesters but couldn't find any. Some clever filmmaker had an opportunity if they could develop an idea. I'd watched every season of *Derry Girls*, so I knew serious topics could be delivered with humor. Since Maggie's death, I realized I kept drifting toward the negative, and I had to stop it, for my sake if no one else's. I hoped to keep my eyes open today for a funny anecdote I could share later.

And didn't *quite* find one.

On light rail, a stocky blond woman in her thirties, sitting next to a stocky blond man and two suitcases, gave me the finger.

"Sorry," I said, "no substitutes."

"Huh?"

"You pimping out your husband?"

She jumped to her feet and leaned forward but stopped as if being held back, though no one was touching her. "We don't like your kind here!"

"This is my city, lady. You're the visitor. Mind your manners."

"It's *my* country."

"Well, it's *my* planet."

That seemed to confuse the woman. Her husband was looking out the window. I expect this wasn't her first public outburst. Social norms had morphed considerably since the pandemic began.

Frankly, I'd never have behaved like this in years past myself.

I'd never tried online "dating" before, either.

I'd hooked up with Doug Stopher, the fuck buddy/fuck activist who'd messaged me online. "Are you okay not using condoms?" he'd asked that first time as he started unbuckling my belt. "Polyurethane is plastic and won't degrade quickly."

I remembered reading John Donne's poem, "The Flea," where a would-be paramour offered an equally ridiculous rationalization.

But when you're sixty-two, already have HIV, and you feel your life is mostly over anyway, going bareback isn't as offputting as perhaps it should be. I'd tested positive just a few months before Toby and I started dating, and we'd always used condoms, though my viral load had been undetectable for over twenty years.

When I was young, I could easily stay hard while wearing a condom. For the past several years, I couldn't feel a thing if I wore a condom, not even a thin one.

Old or not, a guy needed to feel *some* stimulation to stay hard. Even after taking a dick pill.

"As long as we're not using petroleum jelly," I'd replied. Doug had thick, sandy blond hair, with tufts of dark blond wool on his chest and soft, untrimmed pubes around his shaft, bushy enough almost to hide his dick even when erect, despite being close to six inches long.

Real inches, not gay inches.

Some folks might have found him too bushy—I kept thinking of Larry David describing oral sex—but it was just more to bury my face in.

"I use a glycerin-based lotion," he told me. "But I'm also okay with olive oil or coconut oil."

"You look about thirty years old," I said. "How many times can you cum?"

"Twice if I'm motivated."

"Then let's fuck once with lotion and a second time with the coconut oil and see which we like better."

It turned out we liked it both ways. Then I'd fucked him with hair conditioner as lube. That worked well, too, and it was cheaper than silicone. He lay face down, but propped on his elbows, and read the ingredients on the hair conditioner bottle aloud while I pumped away. The behavior was so unexpected it made me harder.

Doug was negative but on PrEP and not worried about my status. His ass was a little flat without being flabby, nowhere near as nice as Toby's. But this was one of the things I loved most about variety…the variety.

As much as I loved boiled peanuts, I wouldn't want to eat *only* boiled peanuts every day.

Doug and I agreed to meet again for another play session.

We'd also agreed to meet today in front of the bank. "If you're as good at protests as you are in bed," Doug told me, "we'll be good buddies."

The bank we were protesting was located on 5th Avenue, though it was hardly the only bank still providing loans for fossil fuel projects. In recent years, many universities had succumbed to pressure to divest their portfolios from fossil fuels. Several municipalities had as well. But some lawmakers were now making divestment a crime.

As I turned the corner onto 5th Avenue, I saw the first of the crowd. Lots of folks wore green shirts. Even more carried signs.

What's Your ROI on Death?

Invest in our Future, Not in Fossils!

Climate Change Is Bankrupting Us!

Oil Companies Drain Climate Savings

Banks Only Succeed if Civilization Survives

A man wearing a green face mask waved at me and I headed toward him. I'd removed my own COVID mask when I stepped off the train, but as Doug greeted me, he leaned over and shouted into my ear to be heard over the crowd. "Always wear a mask at protests. You're on camera."

I dug my mask out of my fanny pack and put it back on.

"So good to see you," he said. "Sometimes, all you have in common with a fuck buddy is a dick."

Most times, I suspected, that was enough.

In fact, after a dick drought lasting years, every drop of dick I could suck up provided lifesaving sustenance. I supposed it was possible to have a deluge of dicks, but climate change hadn't overloaded the atmosphere with too much semen. Yet.

The lyrics to "It's Raining Men" started flowing through my head.

And now I was thinking about things that flowed.

It did feel good to have something in common with Doug. I liked Toby well enough. I think I still loved him. But even close roommates were never quite as close as close spouses, and with no hope now of reestablishing a sexual relationship, our marriage couldn't help but evolve.

"Invest in green energy!" the crowd began chanting. "Invest in green energy! Invest in green energy!"

I remembered how energized I'd felt the day I met Jonah at the flight attendant rally.

Doug waved his sign high in the air. *You Can't Eat Money During a Famine.*

But every rich person in the world always assumed *they'd* have money and shelter and protection, even if everyone else was dying around them. The inability to see reality was part of how addiction worked.

"Nice sign," I said, even if I didn't think it would impact decision makers. It could still impact people who saw it on the news.

Only I didn't see any news crews present.

"No loans for climate killers! No loans for climate killers! No loans for climate killers!"

"Orange skies from wildfires. Orange jumpsuits for the criminals behind them!"

Despite the gravity of the subject, the rally had a party atmosphere. The chanting and sign waving continued another twenty minutes. I was having fun. Doug leaned over to tweak my nipple a couple of times, fingering my nipple ring, and no one seemed to notice. Or care if they did notice.

I wondered if there'd be a speaker, but since we were on the sidewalk, I wasn't sure if the organizers had been granted a permit for that. At one point, a line of protesters held hands and blocked traffic in the street, something clearly not permitted because police swooped in and began arresting those who refused to return to the sidewalk. I pulled out my cell phone and started taking pictures. No violence, thank God, but still something people needed to see.

"Never bring your phone to a protest," Doug said.

"Why? We need to document this."

"Cell phone locations can be traced. Let someone else document the events."

I aimed my camera and took several more photos.

While the police were occupied with detaining the last of the road blockers, I heard the crowd behind us shout, and I turned to see people rushing away from the bank's entrance. It took me a moment to understand what was happening. Someone had poured a huge bucket of used motor oil onto the sidewalk leading up to the doors.

But it wasn't just oil. There were pieces of paper in the oil, completely blackened. It took another moment for me to recognize the size of the paper. The bucket had been filled with oil-covered money. Fake money, probably, but the right size for bills. Perhaps actual $1 bills. It wasn't Monopoly money.

I took a few more pictures.

"Let's go." Doug pulled on my arm and pointed. More police were running toward the crowd and protesters were heading off in all directions.

Throwing oil on the path leading up to the front doors of the bank was obviously *not* something you could get a permit for. Radicals in the crowd were breaking the law. Which meant that to the police, *everyone* in the crowd was breaking the law.

I'd seen the same thing during the George Floyd protests.

Doug dropped his sign, and now I recognized why it might be a good idea to print out slogans on a computer before taping them to posterboard. My sign was covered in my own handwriting. I kept it with me as we ran.

We kept running past City Hall and the courthouse and then through the grimy area near Pioneer Square. I finally dropped my sign near two tents on a small, grass-covered plot, hoping not to aggravate the residents inside them. Doug and I continued jogging on to the International District.

"Whew!" I leaned over, my hand on my side, when we reached Jackson.

I remembered the excited gleam in the eye of the hunter driving his Jeep away from the T-rex in *Jurassic Park.*

"Sorry," Doug said, clapping me on the shoulder. "I forget the difference in our ages."

I gave him a look from my bent over position.

"You're a lot younger in bed."

"Uh huh." I panted a bit longer. "With the lights out? And facing the other way?" I stuck out my tongue.

"You do know that some of the hair around your asshole is gray?"

I laughed. "I need to buy a periscope." I couldn't tell if I was pretending to have a good time or really was. I'd felt disconnected from myself ever since Maggie. But I decided to just go with it. If I was fooling myself, I wanted to be fooled.

"I've got some vegetable dye," Doug said. "We could experiment with different colors back there."

"Why not?" I laughed again. "We're wild and crazy activists."

I sure wished I still had my chaps.

***

I stepped out of the shower and stood in front of the fan in the living room drying off. Not the prettiest sight, since my crotch both fore and aft needed the most attention, but Toby could always head to his office if he didn't want to see. He headed out front instead to check the mail. When he came back, he handed me thick fundraising letters from three different environmental organizations, all wasting money as well as paper, since I responded far better to email requests. The physical letters simply angered me.

Still standing in front of the fan, I took the mail Toby offered.

"Thank you."

"Your hands are chilly," he said.

"You know what they say." I shrugged. "Chilly hands, tepid heart."

I thought I heard him mutter, "It's not your heart that's tepid," as he walked away, but since I had no idea what that might mean, I figured I'd heard wrong. The tone wasn't positive, though, so I thought it best not to seek clarification.

***

It turned out that Doug had several other activist friends, most of them straight or with unclear orientations. One looked trans, but no one said anything, and there was really no reason to ask. Doug said the group met a couple of times a month for Movie Night. There weren't that many climate movies to watch, at least, not narrative films, but they'd watched *Don't Look Up* together, plus *The Trick* and *Beasts of the Southern Wild*. One "fictional" movie they talked about had the title of a true crime show, *How to Blow Up a Pipeline*. I was glad I hadn't seen that one.

Mostly, they watched documentaries. There were plenty of those. But even a grim documentary wasn't as grim as the prospect of terrorism. Throwing a bucket of oil on the sidewalk was one thing. I wasn't daring enough for anything more than that.

To date, my most radical vigilantism involved taking a pair of garden shears and walking around the neighborhood at night trimming branches that blocked free access to the sidewalk, so that people walking their dogs, or folks in wheelchairs, or the mail carrier, could go by without being slapped in the face.

No one was going to make a documentary about *The Night Clipper*.

On Friday, Toby went to meet a friend for dinner, and I went to Doug's to watch *Anthropocene* with his friends.

"Jonah!" I said. The flight attendant gave me a kiss and a big hug. I'd invited him but wasn't sure he'd come. And suddenly, I felt the same energy again that I'd felt at the flight attendant rally and the bank rally. "You okay staying late after everyone else leaves tonight? Doug, you okay with a threeway after the movie?"

"We're fuck activists," Doug explained to Jonah, who seemed to need no further explanation.

"I'm in," he said. Then, wagging his eyebrows, he added, "I'm sensing some double penetration in a certain pal's future." He looked directly at me. It was what he'd whispered in my ear at the end of our first encounter.

***

I had to admit, double penetration looked a lot more fun in porn that it turned out to be in reality. Doug and Jonah took their time opening me up, of course. It was just that the logistics were terribly awkward. Still, I'd always wanted to try it and now I had. From here on, I could concentrate on fulfilling other fantasies.

I'd always wanted to try making a train. Three, four, or five guys fucking in a row.

I could be the engine one time, a freight car the next, the caboose another…

I remembered my father declaring that all gay men were disgusting perverts. "If only that were true," I'd wanted to tell him. "If only that were true."

"You guys didn't really pour oil in front of the bank, did you?" Jonah asked. Apparently, some news crew did film the incident.

"*We* didn't," Doug said, "but I'm glad someone did."

"I don't know. It's like blocking traffic."

"Which we did, too."

"Which some of the others did," Doug corrected me.

Jonah shook his head. "I think maybe it's hurting the cause. People won't get behind things like that."

Doug licked the last of my cum off of Jonah's stomach. "How can our cause be hurt any more than it already is?" he asked. "Every year, more carbon goes up into the atmosphere."

"Still. I don't think it helps when people glue themselves to picture frames in museums or throw tomato soup at paintings."

"They threw the soup at a painting that was protected by glass," Doug reminded him.

I didn't need to be the mind reader to feel a growing tension between the two. Unfortunate, since we'd been so intimate only moments earlier. They weren't really sniping, both speaking calmly. But whether or not they felt the tension, I certainly did.

"Those kinds of things turn people off," Jonah insisted. "I've seen people in the UK glue themselves to the street."

Doug chuckled.

"And even to the tarmac at an airport." Jonah shook his head. "When you delay one flight, it impacts another, which impacts another. A stunt like that can cost millions."

"Exactly the point, isn't it?" Doug asked.

"Flight attendants don't get paid until the door shuts once boarding is complete."

"So you lose a hundred dollars, maybe two hundred. What about people who lose everything they own during a flood?"

"Two wrongs don't make a right."

"Allowing wrong to continue unchallenged doesn't make things right, either. Passivity isn't alchemy."

"I like being passive!" I said, slapping my ass, trying to lighten the mood.

Jonah kissed my hand and then climbed out of bed and started dressing. "I just think there are better ways to get people to address climate change."

"Then for God's sake, do them." Doug still had no snarkiness in his tone, but the words themselves made me cringe. I wanted to walk out of the room. "If you can save the world without offending or inconveniencing anyone, please do it. But I can tell you one thing—I'm not waiting around for you or anyone else to figure out that perfect solution."

Jonah smiled thinly and headed out. On my way home, I heard a ping and read his text. “Let’s watch an airplane movie at my place next time.”

It was exactly what I’d been about to ask him.

To Obey or Not to Obey

I trudged the last block uphill toward home. What had started as a perfectly lovely evening had morphed into disaster in just a few minutes. I wasn't sure Jonah would want to see me again. We'd been watching some flight attendant porn when I got a text from Doug and made the mistake of glancing at it.

I'd never had to ignore texts when spending time with someone before because I so rarely received any messages.

"Fuck!" I'd exclaimed involuntarily.

"What?" Jonah continued slowly stroking himself.

"Doug wants to slash tires on gas guzzlers."

The stroking stopped. "You're not still seeing that jerk, are you?"

"I'm not *seeing* him. We're fucking."

The lights were off at my house. I'd stayed out way too late. That wasn't fair to Toby. We didn't have many rules when we established our open relationship after we got together, but one was never to spend the night with another guy. He had to have gone to bed tonight thinking that was exactly what I'd done.

Jonah and I had gone on to have a long, overly serious discussion about what was and wasn't acceptable in terms of protests and activism.

I'd forgotten how satisfying a meaningful conversation could be, even if it was simultaneously nerve racking.

I could have texted Toby I was running late, should have, yet I hadn't. Probably passive aggressive on my part, not a trait I usually exhibited. But it was hard to get past that limp dick comment.

I wondered how many life-altering decisions had been made by presidents and prime ministers and kings, by CEOs and archbishops and generals, simply because those men were trying to prove something to themselves or others.

I could almost imagine the top guy at an oil company, pissed at his ex-wife after a nasty divorce, thinking, "I'll show *her*. She thinks she'll have a good life without *me*? I'll destroy the whole world!" and then ramping up production.

Surely, money would be the driving force for these jerks, not spite, but lots of men massacred their exes and children rather than accept a breakup. Plenty of evidence out there showing humans did not make rational decisions.

I remembered the time I'd entered the Seattle Leatherman contest years ago because organizers said no one else had entered yet.

I wondered if self-defeating behavior had a genetic component. Why did so many members of our species keep doing it?

It wasn't rational even to use money as a reason to keep increasing carbon emissions. There wasn't *any* logical reason to do so. It might take a while to wind production down, but we could certainly agree not to keep *adding* new fossil fuel projects.

Only we couldn't agree.

I was tired.

Once back inside the house, it suddenly dawned on me that after losing so much weight, my sleep apnea might have abated. I was down to 185. I might be able to try sleeping beside Toby again. That would be nice, even if we didn't have sex.

I paused at Toby's bedroom door. Should I go in and kiss him goodnight so he wouldn't wake up later wondering if I was still out?

I turned the handle softly and opened the door. Toby was fast asleep.

So was the man beside him.

I shut the door quietly and went to sleep as usual on the sofa.

***

On my way to the bus stop, I saw Kaymeena in front of her house, pulling her recycling bin to the curb. "Another wonderfully hot day," I said cheerily.

"Lying's a sin," she said, laughing.

"You don't think it's hot?"

"Sure, but you don't think it's wonderful."

I shrugged. “I find if I use less deodorant, people keep their distance at work.”

Kaymeena laughed again. “If I invite you to hear our youth choir this Sunday,” she said, “will you promise to wear more deodorant?” She tilted her head hopefully, her braids falling to one side. One of them was dyed cobalt blue.

I could hardly think of anything I’d like to do less than go to church, any church, on my day off. Or ever.

“Um, sure.”

She shrugged. “I’m the youth choir director,” she said. “I needed to do something to fit in quickly, and volunteering always helps.”

Fit in quickly? I’d seen Kaymeena and Christopher leave in their church clothes every Sunday for years. “Did you guys get a new pastor?” I asked.

“We got a new church,” she said. “You know Christopher was a deacon and we really liked the congregation. But our pastor there decided everyone in the lay ministry had to sign an anti-LGBTQ pledge, and Christopher refused.”

Dear sweet Jesus.

“So we had to find another place to worship.”

I nodded, trying to look unaffected by the revelation. “What will the kids be singing?”

Kaymeena listed several hymns I’d never heard before, gushing with enthusiasm.

"I'm not sure if Toby's free," I said, "but I'll be there. Text me the time and location."

Kaymeena waved happily and I continued on to the bus stop. We'd be stocking more fake weight loss supplements today at the drugstore.

***

"Another Movie Night?" Toby asked. "Don't you get tired of all the gloom and doom?"

I shrugged. "The gloom and doom is there regardless." My friend Roger had sent me a cartoon this morning featuring a postcard image of a Greek resort. Burning. The caption read, "Having a helluva time. Wish I weren't here."

"But you could watch a comedy instead. Don't you need something fun to stay sane?"

"You and I watch comedies three nights a week," I said. Reruns of *The Vicar of Dibley* right now. Dawn French was always a delight. We'd also watched *Date Night* last Saturday, awkward for obvious reasons, but another enjoyable story. It *was* important to include some light in our lives.

All the Light We Cannot See.

Well, Toby wouldn't want to watch that one.

Toby and I still spent plenty of time together. We simply didn't spend much time talking.

"I'm okay with you having friends," Toby said, "but sometimes I feel like you're distancing yourself. You still love me, don't you?"

I paused. "Toby," I said, "I watched a good friend burn to death. I can't just forget about it. I've got to *do* something."

"Like watch a movie?"

"We—we make plans."

"Craig, Craig, Craig." I heard Cary Grant's voice. And Ryan O'Neal's. Toby closed his eyes and shook his head. "Get involved in something you *can* do something about. You can't do anything about climate."

Not with that attitude, I thought. "Can't I try for a while?"

Toby sighed. "I hear you on the phone with your friends. You want to stop drilling in the U.S."

"New drilling."

I remembered Sarah Palin saying, "Drill, baby, drill!" during a vice presidential debate. I could still see Marjorie Taylor Green's face on January 6 as she gleefully refused a COVID mask while sheltering with vulnerable colleagues during the insurrection. So many millions of people took delight in cruelty, doing the meanest things possible solely out of spite, wanting to make their "enemies"—fellow U.S. citizens—miserable.

Members of my own family had prayed for the Last Days, for God to burn the Earth. They simultaneously didn't believe in global warming *and* saw it as God's promise to cleanse the Earth of people like me.

Toby shook his head again. "It's better to drill our own oil than pay other countries for theirs. Even you have to admit that."

I waited a moment before answering. Democrats might not say the crazy things Republicans did but they still lied to protect their money and political power. Did Toby really believe what he was saying or was he only parroting what some "left-wing" media pundit had said? We couldn't all be experts on everything. We had to take somebody else's word sometimes.

I simply no longer trusted the trustworthiness of "accepted" logic on climate policy.

"I suppose," I said slowly. "Suicide *is* better than being murdered." I paused again. "But are those really our only options? Can't we try to live instead?"

Toby's mouth set, and he paused far longer than I had. "I notice you didn't answer my question."

I knew exactly which question he meant.

"You're welcome to come along if you like."

"No, thanks. I have plans."

***

Only five of us showed up to watch *This Changes Everything*. It wasn't really a movie to cuddle during, but Doug and I cuddled anyway. Sarosh, another activist, looked over at us a few times but not in a particularly perturbed way. Sarosh was short with skin almost as dark as his eyes. He had the start of a pot belly but was so adorable I wanted to hug him from behind and squeeze.

The other two activists there tonight, Miguel and Shawna, both straight, didn't seem to notice at all. When you were facing the end of civilization, I supposed there were more important issues than worrying about what two men might or might not do in bed.

"The problem," Shawna commented after the documentary ended, "is that facts about climate change *don't* change everything. They don't change much of *anything*."

"It takes more than facts," Doug said. "It takes acts."

"A slogan if I ever heard one." Sarosh tapped something into his phone.

We chatted a bit longer about random things, problems at work, meals we planned for later in the week. The complete casualness of the conversation was unexpectedly thrilling, almost making me feel human again.

I remembered Bob Crane in *Auto Focus* proclaiming, "I'm normal!"

Maybe life did go on.

I wanted life to go on.

After a brief comparison of skin tones about the room, Miguel commented on Shawna's purple hair.

"It's lavender," Shawna corrected.

"And lovely." I gave her a thumbs up.

"You have to excuse Miguel," Doug said. "Straight men don't notice colors the same way gay men do."

"Really?" Sarosh asked.

"What color is this?" Doug pointed to his shirt.

"Green?" Miguel guessed. "Green*ish*?"

"Like 'clean' natural gas?" Doug grinned.

"It's sage," I said.

Doug turned back to Shawna. "Straight men only know primary colors."

I thought about all the red baiting these days.

Shawna giggled. "What color is this?" She pointed to her skirt.

"Mauve?" Sarosh tried.

"You must at least be bi," Doug pronounced.

Sarosh blushed but didn't deny it. Maybe I *would* try to squeeze him from behind sometime.

Nothing about the banter was particularly clever. It was simply another Mexi-Coke moment.

Miguel shrugged and got back to important matters. "I'll buy some aqua and salmon-colored markers," he promised. "We need to organize another protest."

We talked about possible dates and times for a few minutes, what other groups we might coordinate with, and then Shawna and Miguel headed back to their apartments. Doug whispered something to Sarosh which made him blush again, and then he was off as well.

"You don't actually want to organize another protest, do you?" I asked. "I can see it in your eyes."

"I bought you something." Doug motioned for me to follow him to the bedroom. It seemed he was done with that conversation. I didn't suppose it mattered, if we were about to have sex. Had he bought us a new toy?

Life almost felt within reach again.

Doug opened a drawer and pulled out a black hoodie and a black pair of jeans and set them on the bed. Both looked pre-worn. He also set a pair of black sneakers on the floor.

Surely, we weren't going to have sex in those. Role play was one thing, but what was that outfit supposed to be?

"Uh…"

"We need clothes no one else has seen us in," Doug explained. "That way, if we show up on someone's surveillance camera, no one who sees a blurry image can say, 'Hey! I think I know who those guys are!'"

"Surveillance camera!" Goddamn. I felt as if my heart literally skipped a beat. I was too old for this kind of thing. I could have a heart attack.

How had we gone from talking about hair to this?

"Tonight, we're going to act." Doug reached over and started tugging off my red T-shirt. "It'll be a small act, but it's still important."

"What are we going to do?" I could feel my left hand trembling and remembered how much I'd trembled the first time I had sex with a man.

Doug gave a tiny shrug. "Just a little spray painting. No real property damage."

I wanted to say no. I knew I should say no. If I got arrested even on a minor charge, I'd probably be fired from my job at the drugstore. Employers weren't eager to hire people my age. And if Toby and I split up, I'd need to be able to keep paying bills on my own.

"Slashing tires takes too long," Doug went on. "And tagging a car makes more of a statement. The tires could just be vandals instead of activists."

Oh my Lord.

"Don't tell Jonah. I know you're still seeing him."

"I'm not *seeing* him. We're fucking."

Doug handed me a pair of black nitrile gloves. "I promise you," he said. "Action is addictive."

Were there 12-step programs for activists?

After we set our phones on Doug's coffee table, we climbed into his car and left his Beacon Hill neighborhood, heading north. "I started buying spray paint and dark clothing months ago," Doug began. "That makes it harder for anyone to track where or when the paint was purchased if the police start looking for us."

"Lord have mercy."

"The clothes I mostly get from thrift stores, so there aren't many cameras."

We passed underneath a stoplight. A sign on the post warned us that the light was monitored by camera to give tickets to anyone who didn't obey traffic rules. "But there are cameras everywhere these days," I said. "How can we get away with anything?"

"Good grief, Craig. Don't you watch the news? People get away with stuff all the time."

I supposed that was true, but I wondered how hard detectives searched for the killer of a gang member or drug dealer. If a wealthy person got on their case about tracking down someone who smudged their car, though, somehow I suspected more resources might go into that investigation.

Of course, I didn't know any police officers or detectives personally. All I knew was what I saw on the news and occasional TV shows. But I also knew I could be in the living room casually mentioning a movie to Toby that I hadn't seen in decades, and minutes later on my computer, an ad pushing a DVD of that movie would pop up. Not even a Blu-ray version but a DVD.

We hadn't activated voice control on our remote, and I wasn't generally a paranoid person, but I was pretty sure our devices were monitoring us. Whether any human ears analyzed that data was one thing, but AI and algorithms certainly did.

We parked under a tree so Doug's car was shielded from the light of streetlamps.

"What kind of tags are we painting?" I asked. "I think I saw a news report about Extinction Rebellion." They used a specific symbol during their actions.

"I hate to co-opt their design," Doug said. "Though I'm not sure they'd mind. Whatever we write has to be quick. And these cans don't really hold much paint. But it can't just be an X. The paint needs to convey a message."

"So…?"

"Tonight, let's just paint the word 'Oil' and then layer an X across it."

"Four letters? That still seems like a lot of paint. And time." We were going to get caught for sure.

I wondered if Toby would even bother bailing me out of jail. Or did you get put in jail for spray painting? Maybe it was only theft that got you physically put in jail while awaiting trial.

I really needed to watch more detective shows.

We started down the street, keeping the cans of spray paint under our hoodies, hot out here even after the sun went down. In years past, I used to wear a light jacket during summer evenings. I hadn't done that in three or four years.

It was late, so not many people were out, but the moment a car drove by or someone came out to walk their dog, we kept walking as if heading somewhere specific. If no one was around, Doug pointed out vehicles shaded from streetlamps by tree canopies.

Even if someone appeared unexpectedly, they wouldn't notice us unless they were only a few feet away.

Doug and I each tagged ten cars before the cans started fizzling out. "Let's go," I said. "That's enough for one night." No need to push our luck.

I'd never been a "bad boy." In high school, I'd been voted "Most Likely to Be Polite" my senior year.

Even when I got my nipple piercing twenty-five years ago and been pulled over for not wearing a seatbelt, I'd apologized profusely, hoping to avoid my first ticket. "I'm sorry, officer, but the strap runs right across my new nipple piercing and makes it bleed." I'd pulled up my T-shirt to show him.

I got a ticket anyway. But then I used the story when I competed for Seattle Leatherman to show how butch I was.

Even with no competitors, I still lost.

Of course, that was many years ago. I felt a bit of a thrill now as we headed back to Doug's car. After I fastened my seatbelt, Doug exited again. "Forgot something," he said. He went around back and opened the trunk. Then it sounded like he was walking away somewhere behind the car.

Surely, he wasn't spraying more paint, was he? So frustrating. With no transportation of my own, I was trapped, my lack of funds an anchor.

The driver's side door opened suddenly, and Doug jumped into the seat, shoving his key into the ignition.

"What? Did someone see you?"

Doug didn't answer but pulled away quickly. We'd hardly driven fifteen feet when there was a flash behind us and the sound of a small explosion.

"What the hell!" I couldn't turn around without hurting my neck. Old tendons. "What did you do!?"

"Molotov cocktail in the tailpipe of a particularly nasty gas guzzler."

We turned a corner and kept driving, at a normal speed now so as not to attract attention.

"If we can inspire more people to tag and burn cars," Doug said, "we can make it too risky for insurance companies to insure them, the way they already won't insure homes in some states because of flooding and wildfires."

"Oh my God."

I'd agreed to deface property but was now an accessory to the destruction of property. *Expensive* property. That was undoubtedly a felony.

"Don't tell Toby," Doug advised. "Or Jonah."

I couldn't even say it out loud to myself anyplace where a phone or TV or computer might overhear. No looking up news articles online about the incident, either. Nothing.

Things had sure escalated quickly, I realized, too late.

Just like climate breakdown.

Smoke

Tens of thousands of birds in Missouri and Arkansas died from the heat, their bodies rotting in yards and fields and parking lots.

Two children in Texas, a child in Alabama, and a child in Illinois died after being left in their parents' cars in the blazing sun.

A man was shot and killed after breaking a car window to rescue a dog that had passed out in the heat.

Climate scientists revealed that two-thirds of Morocco's oases had disappeared over the past few decades.

Right-wing politicians banned abortion in state after state. Right-wing pundits called for the stoning of adulterers, for public executions of LGBTQ folks and anyone who supported LGBTQ folks.

Drivers in the UK cursed Just Stop Oil protesters who blocked the street and dared to inconvenience them on their way to the office.

Two climate protesters were shot and killed while blocking a road in Panama.

In Florida, teachers were instructed to teach that slavery taught kidnapped Africans useful skills.

Seventy-five police officers and sheriff's deputies in Pittsburgh went on paid leave during an investigation after firing several thousand rounds at an unarmed man being evicted.

City of Seattle workers had been bargaining for a new contract for over a year and a half, but the mayor and city council refused to offer more than a 1% Cost-of-Living-Adjustment in the face of 16% inflation.

A world-famous musician stopped his concert in mid-song to inform the audience that trans people were unnatural.

Trouble in Paradise…and Limbo and Hell

"What are you plotting, Craig?" Toby looked at me with slightly narrowed eyes, his lips pulled a bit tight.

"What do you mean?"

"I've never seen you pick at your fingernails like that." He nodded toward me. "Your finger's bleeding."

I looked at my hand and stopped picking. I'd caught the edge of one fingernail with another and kept worrying it until I'd torn it to the quick.

What could I tell Toby that wouldn't make everything worse? This wasn't Fight Club, but to tell anyone what I'd done, whether we were on good terms or not, gave them too much power over me.

I shrugged. "It was something Doug said."

"Doug." Toby's sigh wasn't weary but annoyed. "You planning to leave me for him?"

"Nope."

"Then why do you care what he says? He doesn't matter."

As awkward as Toby's direct question had been, I was impressed he was addressing the tension and not simply ignoring it. He'd had *Bodies* on this morning while I was getting ready for work, and I'd watched as Toby pressed the

Forward button any time a conversation onscreen grew too serious.

"Remember the guy a few years ago," I said, "who disrupted an auction for oil rights? I think maybe it was in Nevada."

"No." Toby reached for his phone and checked his texts, though there'd been no ping alerting him of anything incoming.

"He spent years in prison for peaceful civil disobedience."

Toby looked back up at me. "Are you letting Doug get you mixed up in something?" he asked. "I won't have you dragging *me* into anything. I don't want cops showing up *here*."

It took me a moment to catch my breath.

Why did those words hurt so much? Toby's position was perfectly reasonable. *I* didn't want any trouble, either. It had always been the case that not everyone could commit to a high level of civil disobedience with its very real consequences. That didn't make them bad people.

Wasn't I considering breaking off my friendship with Doug for that very reason?

But what if there was no way to successfully battle climate change through the legal system? People with money made the laws and paid others to enforce them. "Justice" only existed from a specific perspective—that of the rich.

"You're picking at your finger again."

Fuck.

I took a couple of slow breaths and then faked a casual shrug. “Doug said some mean things the other day, so I’m just processing. No big deal.”

“Dump him.” Toby turned to his phone again. “You don’t need that kind of stress in your life.” He looked up at me again. “Want me to have some boiled peanuts waiting for you when you get home?”

***

“Ever have sex in a flight simulator?” Jonah asked. “They have one at the Museum of Flight.”

“Isn’t that monitored?”

“Your point?”

“I think I’ll pass.”

The morning after the Molotov cocktail incident, one of the first ads to show up on my computer was for car insurance. Not overly suspicious, but since I hadn’t driven in two decades, oddly non-targeted. Only a few minutes later, though, another ad appeared, this one for a national brand of spray paint.

I supposed cars had ears, too. And it wasn’t even my car.

I hated thinking like this, but if you were going to do risky, illegal things, perhaps it didn’t hurt to be paranoid.

“Then you’ll need to strap yourself into my loveseat.” Jonah pointed. He walked over to the closet and pulled out a small blanket with a rival airline’s logo before dimming the lights. "We'll be two passengers on a red eye getting to know each other while everyone else sleeps."

The scenario was cliché and ridiculous, but my dick twitched just at the suggestion.

I felt like Robert DeNiro in *Awakenings*. I hadn't exactly been in a coma for years, but my dick had certainly been in a vegetative state. And coming back to life didn't always proceed smoothly. Expect problems, I warned myself.

I supposed I was a dick half full kind of guy.

But I still eagerly joined Jonah on the loveseat.

Of course, the reality was that giving each other handjobs while still clothed turned out to be rather messy. Some of Jonah's cum ended up on his chest and the blanket, but mine ended up on the outside of my jeans at crotch level.

"Got anything to wipe this up with?" I asked after we stopped kissing.

Jonah shook his head. "You should head to the grocery on your way home," he suggested, "and see who looks. That way you'll know who to proposition."

And damn it if *those* words didn't get my worn-out dick to twitch yet again.

"When's your next flight?" I asked.

"Tomorrow at 7:00 a.m." He pulled me up and wiped my pants off with the airline blanket. "To Oklahoma City, then Dallas, and back. Shouldn't be too bad. Unless there's weather." He left my dick hanging out of my pants. His own remained hanging out, too.

This was the way all conversations should be conducted.

But when Jonah stuck his arms out to his sides in a straight line and then started tilting right and left, making engine noises like a little kid, I remembered a scene from *The Day After Tomorrow* where an airplane crashes. The film had left an impression, despite its scientific inaccuracies. "Do you get much rough weather?"

"Pilots are good at avoiding it, but we do have more flights canceled these days because of storms. Sometimes, we can only avoid the turbulence by not flying at all."

"And you don't get paid when a flight's canceled?"

"That's right."

"Does that make you *want* to fly even if the weather is bad?" A last drop of cum had formed on the tip of Jonah's penis, and I reached down to wipe it off with my finger. Rather than lick my finger, though, I dabbed the spot on my moustache right beneath my nose and inhaled.

"Gotta pay the bills, don't I?"

Like farm workers keeling over in 100-degree heat.

"Flights are canceled for smoke, too," Jonah added. "And sometimes for heat. When it gets really hot, the air's too thin to give the plane enough lift for takeoff."

I looked down at my own dick, but it was bone dry. "You ever think about putting flyers on windshields in the parking lots at other airports?"

"And say what? 'Stop flying and put me out of a job'? I *like* what I do."

I wondered if I should buy some spray paint.

What I really wanted was a can of whipped cream. The real kind. The body parts you could lick that off of…

And out of.

"Do *you* put out flyers about the greed of drug companies in the parking lot at your drugstore?" Jonah asked.

I chuckled. He was right, of course. Always easier to point out what *other* people should do. "Text me when you get home tomorrow night," I said. "And we'll do something morally compromising in bed that'll keep us from thinking about any other moral compromises we make."

How in the world at my age I still had enough testosterone flowing through my system to keep me horny after cumming was enough of a miracle. I didn't need to shoot for the moon.

I remembered the days when I actually could shoot and not just dribble. I was doing exercises after watching a YouTube video, but…

"Promise?" Jonah asked, kissing my cheek.

"I've already got three ideas and I'm working on a way to combine all of them."

"I'll be pissed if our flight home gets delayed."

"There might be piss involved either way." When Jonah raised an eyebrow, I finished zipping up as casually as possible. "Just saying."

I was already taking for granted the two new men in my life who were both ten times more interested in sex than Toby had ever been.

Well, than he'd ever been with *me*.

I was Jed Clampett, dirt poor one day and living in luxurious Beverly Hills the next.

I wanted to be Elly May. Or maybe even Granny. She didn't tolerate any nonsense.

"You're trouble, Craig," Jonah said. "T-R-O-U-B-L-E. Right here in Emerald City."

And damn if my dick didn't twitch again.

Tin Foil

I woke up sometime after midnight when I heard Toby leaving his office in the back of the house. He stopped in the bathroom a moment, turned out the light over the stove, and then headed into the living room on his way to the bedroom.

I started patting my lap as an invitation. I still liked to rub his back before bed maybe once a week. The lamp was on in his bedroom, casting a dim light into the living room, but after leaving his brightly lit office and the bathroom, Toby's eyes hadn't adjusted yet.

He stiffened when he heard me patting my lap and turned toward me, hesitating a moment. I continued patting, and he slowly made his way toward me, reaching out in the darkness. He turned around and backed toward me as I kept up my efforts at echolocation, and he sat down, missing the center of my lap and then adjusting his position in the dark.

The slight grind made me want to press myself up into him. Knowing he didn't want me to made my heart ache.

I started rubbing his back, suddenly realizing that in our entire marriage, he'd never rubbed my back even once. Still, I did like rubbing his. Reciprocity came in different ways. After maybe five minutes, Toby stood up to continue on to his bedroom. "Sweet dreams, Craig," he whispered.

***

I didn't know why I bothered. My life was too complicated as it was, but I needed to try moving away from Doug, and the only way I saw to force myself was to reach out to someone else. I messaged three other guys on the hookup sites I was on. Two never responded, not even a thanks but no thanks. One guy agreed to a video chat. Awkward, but I used the email I created specifically for the account so he could send the link, and I gave it a shot.

Alex was sixty, good looking, about my height, probably ten pounds lighter, and with darkish gray hair that still somehow almost looked luminescent.

He'd been with his husband for twenty years, divorced a year ago, and still lived with the guy because both their names were on the mortgage.

"Marcus remarried, and we all live together," Alex informed me. "So I can't host."

He lived in Federal Way and didn't get to Seattle often. "But if I'm up that way, I'll shoot you a message."

And that was that.

I headed over to Doug's to rim him while he beat off. Then he slapped a handful of cum against my asshole and pushed it inside me with his fingers.

Back home, I messaged two other guys.

Hope was cruel.

***

It was 85 degrees when I got home from work. Customers always seemed more irritable in hot weather.

I felt irritable pretty much all the time.

And Toby hadn't watered the front yard in ages. Standing so long aggravated his arthritis. I turned on the hose and started spraying a large area around the trunk of our service berry tree trying to reach all its roots, sweeping back and forth over and over to let the water seep into the ground.

We needed that tree to block some of the afternoon sun or the house would be blazing inside.

I heard a door open and saw Kaymeena step onto her porch. She stretched out her arms in ecstasy.

"I bet you hate this," she said, laughing.

"Hate is a strong word," I said. "And yes, I do."

"Wait just a second." She darted back into her house and returned a moment later. "I bought you some sugar-free frozen yogurt." She walked over and handed it to me. "I wasn't sure what flavor to get, but you seem like a vanilla kind of guy."

***

Last week, I'd left a card on Toby's desk for him to find in the morning after I left for work. An image of a waterfall in the woods. I'd written on the inside, "Thanks for being you." It felt disingenuous to say anything else. But I wanted to salvage something from the relationship. He never even mentioned it when I got home, and I didn't say anything, either.

Today at work, just as I was finishing my lunch break, I decided to send Toby a short text. Nothing special. Perhaps "I'm thinking about you," but that almost begged the question. "What is Craig thinking about me? Planning a divorce?"

So I took a gamble and texted, "I love you."

Then I got back to work.

A few minutes later, I could hear a ping on my phone and knew Toby must have texted back. It made me smile. At least he'd acknowledged my effort this time. I didn't have time to respond, no time even to look at my phone, busy waiting on customers while Kellyn took her lunch.

A few minutes after the first ping, I heard another, and a minute later, yet another.

What was going on? Had I upset him? Did Toby not want me to say I loved him anymore? I stole a glance at my phone.

"Are you OK?"

"You OK?"

"Answer!"

"Craig!"

No customers were in sight, and neither was my manager, so I hit Toby's number.

"Oh my god!" he said. "You scared me!"

"Huh?"

"That's the kind of text you send when you're being killed in a mass shooting."

Edamame pasta and tomato sauce were waiting for me when I got home. And a gentle kiss.

***

We turned off our phones, put them in a box, and left them in the kitchen. Doug didn't have either a TV or computer in his bedroom, and we sat on his bed with the door closed. Music played in the living room to help drown out any conversation that might still be detected through the door.

I felt like a QAnon fanatic.

Did we need to start wearing tin foil hats?

"It's been over a week," Doug said. "I'm sure the police are still looking, but there's nothing more in the news about what we did. I think we're okay for now."

"It's good for my diet, anyway." I tried to chuckle, but it came out as more of a cough. "Normally, I'd be stress eating or eating out of boredom, but I've been too nervous to eat at all."

"Craig, you look fine. Don't buy into the fat shaming."

There were more important things than looking good, more important things than sex. A few days ago, Toby had bought me a DVD of *The Last of Us*, even though he hated all the space my DVDs took up, because he knew owning copies of great shows meant something to me.

I'd bought him some real bread, a loaf of rosemary diamante, so he could slice himself toast in the morning. Toby sighed louder at his first bite than he ever had after an orgasm. He'd been keeping bread out of the house in solidarity for the past couple of years, but I told him he had to do what worked for him, too.

"Remember the hiker whose arm got caught under a boulder?" Doug flexed his left arm.

I vaguely remembered a movie starring James Franco in a fictionalized version of the grim story.

"There came a point when he knew his arm was lost one way or another." Doug examined his arm and I couldn't help but look, too. I was reminded how attractive the hair pattern was. "The question was whether he could save the rest of himself."

And the guy chopped his arm off with a knife, if I remembered correctly, and then hiked to safety. Most people would have chosen death, I realized, either consciously or by postponing the decision to amputate until it was too late.

"I've bought six cans of spray paint at two different stores," I said proudly. "Shopping out in Federal Way and up in Edmonds." Those trips took a very long time on public transit, and Toby was convinced I was out fucking around.

And I was, just not on those trips. So I didn't correct him. Better that than suspecting illegal activities.

"Excellent." Doug pulled me close for a quick peck. "And I've been buying drones."

Another escalation.

"What are you going to do?"

"We're not Texas or Louisiana or Oklahoma," Doug said, "but we still have a few oil and gas refineries here."

"And you're going to drop paint on them?" I really didn't understand strategy one iota. "Maybe we could drop leaflets."

Doug glanced toward the bedroom door and then toward the window. The blinds were down so no one could read our lips, but if anyone was listening with special equipment, I knew they could hear us. In the movies, there were always men in vans filled with monitors outside the suspect's house.

We hadn't done anything to warrant *that*, thank goodness, but Doug's behavior worried me regardless.

"I don't know how to make bombs," he whispered, "but I know where to buy a few."

I put my hand on the bed to steady myself, feeling lightheaded, a slight ringing in my ears. What the hell had I gotten myself into?

What would Doug do to me if I said I wanted no part of it? Would I be a liability? Someone who "knew too much"?

Que sera sera.

"Can't…can't we start with…with mailing envelopes with white powder?" I stammered. "Put a little flour in with a message demanding we stop new oil production?"

"You want to send a *letter*?"

"S—something to keep people on edge but that doesn't *hurt* anyone."

"It's still a criminal offense, Craig. It'll still put us in prison."

"Oh my Lord."

"So why not do something more effective right from the start? We may not get many chances."

I supposed even eighty-year-olds didn't like hearing a diagnosis of terminal cancer. We all wanted just a few more good years. And *this* was like injecting myself with drug-resistant HIV, like inhaling tuberculosis bacteria.

I wasn't ready.

I thought of the song by Carol Lynn Pearson.

"Something like that could kill people," I said. "It could damage the environment."

"So we just buy a case of glue?"

"Well…"

"People see 'stunts' and dismiss us as ineffective. They see that kind of theater—and *not* 19,000 people being evacuated off the island of Rhodes—as drastic."

"Can't we start with the least problematic?"

"We started with the least problematic decades ago."

Was this why suicide bombers killed themselves? Because it was easier than facing the aftermath of what they'd done?

Oh my God. Was I a *terrorist* now?

I just wanted to go to a rally!

"Remember Paradise?" Doug asked. "Remember Lytton? An entire town burning down every couple of years is horrific enough, but we'll soon start to see this kind of thing happen two or three or four times a year." He grabbed both my hands and squeezed. "Things are bad," he said. "But they're not going to *stay* bad."

I sighed.

"They're going to get worse."

I was trembling as if it were twenty degrees in Doug's bedroom. But it wasn't. Like most Seattleites, he didn't own an air conditioner, and it was probably close to eighty in the apartment. "Why are you telling me all this?" I asked. "I can't help with the drones. Why are you making me an accessory?"

Doug dropped my hands and climbed off the bed, staring at the closed bedroom door. "You're right," he said. "It's selfish of me." He turned back and forced a grin. "I suppose it's part of the human condition. I just needed someone I cared about to know. I'm sorry."

I lay in bed with Doug for the next two hours, but we didn't have sex, though I'd douched and showered before coming over. We simply held each other, not saying a word.

I could still hear music from the living room. Dolores O'Riordan was singing about dreams.

Fire

Another nine people were shot, three of them killed, near a bus stop where I usually waited after my shift at the drugstore to get home.

A woman in Virginia was kicked out of a theater restroom with her fifteen-year-old autistic son when the owner accused the boy of being trans rather than disabled.

When news reports out of Florida and Texas covered stories of parents getting new jobs and moving out of state to protect their trans kids, right-wing pundits giggled on air, giddy over the misery they'd created.

Public health officials reported rising cases of malaria and leprosy in the U.S.

A gunman in Memphis was killed trying to break into a yeshiva to conduct a mass shooting.

A man at a Republican political rally shouted into the microphone a reporter offered him, "Kill the left! Kill the RINOs! Kill the globalists!"

Screenwriters had been on strike for months already and now actors were striking, too, demanding royalties for streaming and protection against AI.

Scientists recorded the hottest July ever, the warmest weather the planet had seen in 125,000 years.

For Whom the Siren Tolls

I wondered what Maggie would think of my behavior these past few weeks. Would she be pleased? Horrified? Disappointed I hadn't done more? Upset I was committing criminal acts in her name?

Did it matter what she would have thought?

I felt it did. I wasn't "getting involved" solely to honor her, but I did want her death—and her life—to have mattered. We'd had such fun studying together, running tests to figure out what bacteria we'd been assigned in our Microbiology lab, catching, pinning, and identifying insects in our Entomology class. She got my jokes about squamous cells and I got her jokes about batrachotoxin.

She was the only friend I'd made in college. We hadn't even spent all that much time together. And then after we moved to different cities, we mostly chatted by phone or emailed every couple of months. It was just that she felt like family, close even while apart.

How many other families were being torn apart by climate change?

It wasn't okay.

So ridiculous that such a declaration even needed to be made.

***

I walked over to Kubota Garden before Toby was even awake and sat at one of the picnic tables in the upper part of the garden. I could hear traffic on Renton Avenue and see small planes flying to and from Boeing Field, but I still felt I was in the mountains far away from civilization.

It was peaceful here, and I needed peace. Even folks complaining about the locked bathrooms across from the picnic tables didn't bother me.

I took out a piece of paper and wrote the first draft of an op-ed. "We Need a General Strike Against Fossil Fuels." It wasn't bad, but would any corporate newspaper publish it? Even if an independent online publication posted it, would anyone organize to *do* it?

And was penning an op-ed, even if I could write the best one ever, really an *action*?

I understood Doug's need to do more than talk. But when I went back home, I revised the piece a couple more times and sent it off.

Still feeling antsy, I caught the Sounder to Olympia and bought two paintball guns, along with enough paint to win a tournament. Toby would kill me if he knew how much I'd withdrawn from savings to make the purchase. We'd always maintained separate finances, but it still felt like a betrayal to make any purchase of more than fifty or sixty dollars without discussing it first.

Paintball paint wouldn't permanently stain clothing. Or cars or buildings, for that matter. But forcing people to think about their behavior could still be useful.

Wasn't wishful thinking the flaw that had allowed the climate to deteriorate so much to begin with?

I wanted to do *some* kind of "act" without telling either Doug or Jonah, certainly without telling Toby. Since this would be my first offense, perhaps I'd get off easy and still get to use the experience as a platform to speak out publicly.

And maybe getting jailed for a few months would keep me away from Doug long enough to clear my head and avoid *real* prison time.

I couldn't just target expensive gas guzzlers, though. I needed to target people. Activists had thrown red paint on folks wearing mink and other furs so often that the public finally started turning away from killing animals for their fur. Lots of people still did wear fur, of course. And I still loved leather. But that years-long campaign *had* made a difference.

Doug said it was important to make these kinds of purchases months before the materials were used, to make them harder to trace. But I needed to do something *now*.

How about stickers? It required a bit of vulnerability, but it was impossible to accomplish anything meaningful without taking on *some* risk. Back home on my computer, I looked up a print shop, used some templates from the company's website, and ordered 2000 bumper stickers.

$\uparrow CO_2$ = *Mass Extinction*

I did use a VPN, but I expected this was still easily traceable. Of course, I could always say someone stole the package from my front porch and I never saw them.

Or I could accept my lumps if I was caught.

Those stickers would look great on bumpers. On the door or hood of a car. Even on someone's office door. They'd work anywhere, really.

I still hadn't *done* anything on my own yet, but just being this far into the process satisfied the itch, and I was able to relax for the rest of the day. I called my friend Roger in San Francisco, who informed me he was planning to leave the city. "Not a single store is left open on Market Street," he said. "The city is dying. Homeless people on every block."

Roger and I had met years ago during a deaf performance of *A Streetcar Named Desire*. I'd learned some ASL while dating an early boyfriend but wasn't fluent enough for most of my subsequent conversations with Roger, so we usually relied on TTY relay.

I didn't know where to suggest he go. Things were bad pretty much everywhere. I felt awkward knowing the relay operator was listening to our conversation, as if I was saying something treasonous.

"The Prime Minister of Andorra just came out as gay," I said, "and it's a lovely little country."

"If you don't mind the cold." He typed "LOL," which the relay operator read aloud.

"I wouldn't bet on it staying *too* cold." I'd read recently that the average yearly temperature there had risen more than five degrees Fahrenheit over the past century.

"I'd have to learn two languages," Roger went on. "The written language and an entirely new sign language."

I hadn't considered that.

"I'll probably just move to Mendocino," Roger said. "Still gotta make a living."

I cooked scalloped potatoes for dinner, one of Toby's favorites, even if I could only eat a small serving. He looked at me suspiciously, and I wondered if we were already at the point where we could no longer make simple gestures for one another without an ulterior motive.

After dinner, I moved the coffee table out of the way, pulled the ottoman over, and had Toby sit in front of me while we watched an episode of *This Is Pop* as I rubbed his back. I hit Pause twenty minutes in when he answered a text.

"Maybe we can go hiking on Mount Si some weekend," I suggested before unpausing the show.

"Maybe."

"Is there something else you'd like to do?" I continued rubbing.

"Mmm. Something closer to home?"

"We could take the ferry to Vashon and back. That's always fun."

Toby was silent a moment. "Sure," he finally said. "Let's do that sometime." He shot off another text, and we resumed watching the program.

After he went to his office at the back of the house, I sat at my computer, staring at the screen. I browsed profiles a few minutes, propositioned a guy, and stared at my screen again.

I wanted to call Doug. Or Jonah. Or both.

I beat off instead.

It was the one time I didn't like cum—after cumming. The reaction was probably encoded in my DNA. And probably the only reason I even needed to bother hooking up at all.

I saw a Nobel Prize in some gay geneticist's future.

***

I supposed it should have been obvious. Fun and relaxation didn't go well with serious discussions. I thought perhaps I could slip some ideas into the conversation if I used the lubricant of play. Early in our relationship, Toby and I used to play Scrabble almost weekly. Then once a month, then a few times a year.

We hadn't played Scrabble now in over two years.

"A one," Toby said, reading off the value on the first tile he picked to see who would go first.

"I've got a one, too."

"Another one," he said, choosing his next tile.

I picked another tile from the bag. "A ten," I said.

He laughed. "Your first word should be good!"

It really wasn't, only four letters. Z-I-T-S. Still, it was fun to use a Z without worrying if the word including it would fit on the board before being blocked by another word.

Freedom!

I casually mentioned a news report about a woman forced to carry a brainless fetus to term. Toby had little to say about it. We both played a few more words. I casually mentioned some flooding in France.

Toby made no comment at all.

"Wanna watch something on Kanopy later?" I asked.

"Like what?"

The Naked Jungle had popped into my mind recently, though it was hardly a classic, and I suggested it now. "It's about army ants in Brazil eating everything in their path."

"Sounds charming." Toby didn't sound charmed and didn't look up from the board as he put down S-H-I-N.

"They blow up a dam to flood their farm and drown the ants, but some get through and they still have to burn all their furniture to keep them away." I added a G-L-E to Toby's last word.

"Can't we watch a comedy?" He added an S to my addition. I wondered if he meant the roofing tile or the painful outbreak.

"Sure," I said. "Why not?" I could always watch the other on my own. Toby and I had always been able to pursue separate interests. It's why our marriage had survived so long to begin with. I couldn't help but wonder, though, if we were soon going to be doing *everything* separately.

But I did want to watch the movie, wanted to watch a couple in a strained marriage go all out to save their lives, to save at least their house. Even if they lost everything else, there'd still at least be something to start over with. And the battle would help them finally forge a bond.

"Jumping Jehoshaphat," I said.

"What?"

"I can use all seven of my letters. I've never done that before." A couple of times, I'd had a great word but there hadn't been space on the board for it. We were early enough in the game that the letter I needed to complete my word was right out in the open.

I placed my tiles carefully. I-N-D-O-L-E-N-T. 22 points. Plus 50 bonus points.

"I guess we know who's going to win this game," Toby said. He tried for a neutral tone, and he wasn't mad. But he was disappointed.

No more climate talk for a while. Over the next several turns, I casually mentioned Lampedusa struggling with the influx of 7000 immigrants in a single week and a coup in Niger. I also carefully played words on the board that gave Toby a chance to use two of the triple word score spaces.

I couldn't be obvious about it. No one wanted to be the kid the parent had to "let" win. The truth was that Toby was naturally good at strategy and would likely have caught up to my score anyway, but I didn't want it to take too long. He was being generous to play the game with me again when I asked, and I could certainly let him enjoy himself.

We hadn't had fun for the sake of fun in a very long time.

Toby spelled Q-U-E, thinking it was the spelling for "queue."

"Not bad." I mentioned another story about stormy weather, this time in South Korea.

Toby sighed.

"Wish I had an A." I held my tray of tiles and frowned.

"Yeah?"

"There's a really great word to be made somewhere near the top of the board," I said. "Hope I get an A in my next draw."

Was that too obvious?

Toby studied the board for over a minute and then placed an A on a triple word score space right above the word W-A-K-E going down vertically.

I laughed. "How did neither of us see that until now?"

We continued playing. Years ago, I'd bought a second set of tiles and added them in so that we'd always run out of space on the board before we ran out of good letters to use. By the time we'd been playing almost ninety minutes, we both had scores just over 300. I threw in a couple more news stories about climate, a protest here, a lawsuit there, misery both here and there.

"People need to accept reality," Toby said. "Things aren't going to get better. We just need to put up storm shutters and buy sump pumps for our basements and do the best we can to get by. The government's not going to do anything. It's a waste of time and energy trying."

We had, in fact, bought a window unit for the living room last summer. We couldn't afford to cool the entire house, and he'd suggested we cool the living room rather than the bedroom because he knew I had a harder time falling asleep in the summer than he did.

"It's a waste of emotional energy, too," he continued. "I don't have enough to spare."

"Fighting back can be energizing, though, can't it?" I wrote down the tally from Toby's latest word.

I mentioned a news story about three Asian families in the neighborhood who'd all been traumatized recently by home invasions. One homeowner had been tazed by the intruders.

Toby glanced at his watch.

It was now or never, I supposed. "You fight for your life by any means necessary," I insisted. "If someone breaks into your house, you pull out a baseball bat or a gun. When there's a mass shooting, you run, you hide, or you fight back."

Toby studied the board, scrunching up his nose. There wasn't much space left. "Eleven inches of rain isn't the end of the world."

Parts of Massachusetts were experiencing a "200-year flood" as we played. No one had been killed but there was lots of damage. I'd brought up the story over half an hour earlier. Toby had acted as if he hadn't even heard me.

"Remember a few years back when I almost had a nervous breakdown?" I asked. Toby had refused to start taking his Social Security, even though at sixty-seven he faced no penalties for doing so. My question was a non sequitur. And a touchy subject.

I felt like Elle Woods talking about wet T-shirt contests. I had a point.

"You should be strong enough to pay your bills without needing my money." Toby's lips were pulled tight again. We'd either finish the conversation in the next few seconds or he'd be walking out of the room. He was fifteen points ahead, so at least there was that.

Of course, I paid the electric and water bills by myself, with no contribution from him, so they weren't technically *my* bills. He had a car payment, he always pointed out, so it was only fair that I take on more of the household bills.

"But I *wasn't* strong enough," I said. "People are fragile. And when they lose their cars or their homes or their businesses to flooding, it doesn't matter if eventually their insurance company pays. They're falling to pieces right now."

"What do you want me to do about it?"

"Giving a damn wouldn't hurt."

"It won't help, either."

"Toby," I said, trying to sound casual as I studied the few remaining options on the board before us. "The annual cost of climate disasters in the U.S. is almost 150 billion dollars." I'd looked up some figures for my op-ed the other day. "The entire budget for the U.S. Department of Education is only 70 billion. You could add in the budget for the Coast Guard and the national parks, and you'd still have over 60 billion dollars left over."

I could have made up any numbers and wasn't sure I'd remembered them correctly to begin with. But the basic point was the same.

Toby gave me a raspberry. "You can prove any point with statistics." He put an X on the board below an O. "That doesn't mean anything. Even if we stopped using oil overnight, there'd still be weather disasters. You're not going to be able to get that money back."

I added his latest tally to the scoring sheet. "But we can stop it from becoming 200 billion dollars a year, or 250 billion, or 300 billion."

Toby took a deep breath. "Craig, you're making me miserable. You're making yourself miserable. I realize you just saw a good friend die, but you've got to get some counseling. You're falling apart and I won't have you dragging me down with you."

With all the talk in the news about anchor babies, I'd never considered I might have become an anchor man.

I thought about Will Ferrell.

Toby sighed again. "What's the score?"

I picked up the sheet. "417 to 384." I'd started to catch up again before he put that last word on the board.

It looked like we wouldn't be playing again for a long while.

Neither of us could afford to rent another place while still making payments on this one. But we probably needed a trial separation. There was no way around it. I'd have to see if I could move in temporarily with Jonah. Doug was too scary. Or maybe I could ask if Toby had any friends he could stay with for a few weeks or months. Perhaps his sleepover friend, Martin.

I started putting tiles back in the velvet bag. Toby helped. He usually hated this part and let me do it by myself. But today, he stayed until we'd put everything back.

"We probably only have five halfway decent years left," Toby said. I wasn't sure if he was referring to our age or our relationship or the climate or what. "I don't want to spend them in prison."

That was a perfectly reasonable, perfectly sane, position. *Why did it infuriate me so?*

"I love you, Craig." Toby paused. "I think. But I'll still turn you in if you're doing anything illegal."

I heard David Cassidy singing my favorite Partridge Family song.

And walked to my office to pack an overnight bag.

Gloom

Over 420,000 Americans were now allergic to red meat and dairy after tick bites caused them to experience extreme immune responses to certain proteins.

Changing weather patterns allowed pine beetles to spread hundreds of miles beyond their historical range, turning huge swaths of land into "ghost forests."

A wildfire decimated almost 100,000 acres in Joshua Tree National Park, killing up to a million trees.

Half a billion shellfish on the beach in British Columbia died in just a few hours during low tide in the middle of a heatwave.

Olive trees in Spain, Italy, and Greece began dropping their fruit early to protect themselves against heat and drought.

The home of an Indian family was torched by an arsonist in Federal Way, just south of Seattle, while they slept. They all made it out alive.

An overcrowded boat sank off the coast of Greece, killing 700 migrants, but more people seemed fixated by the news of a tiny submarine carrying five rich people who died when the vehicle imploded deep below the surface while touring the wreckage of the Titanic.

Christian nationalists in Oklahoma, South Carolina, and Texas pushed for a ban on trans care and counseling for adults in addition to existing bans for teens.

Hotel workers in Los Angeles went on strike. Municipal workers in Portland, Oregon went on strike, too.

News organizations revealed that over thirty climate journalists had been murdered in the last decade.

The secretary general of the United Nations declared that "the era of global boiling has arrived."

Kicking against the Pricks

"It's nice of you to let me stay the night."

I'd kept repeating Dylan Thomas's famous mantra on my way over. *Rage, rage against the dying of the light*. But I'd calmed down by the time I arrived.

Doug gave me a kiss and ushered me into his apartment. I'd tried Jonah first, but he was out of town. His flight from Dallas to Oklahoma City had been canceled and he couldn't finish his route back until tomorrow.

"I'm afraid I have a date tonight," Doug said.

"I can put headphones on and stay in the living room."

Doug laughed. "We're okay being heard if you're okay hearing."

"Oh, um, sure." I really just wanted to watch a movie. Something *not* grim. Maybe *Encanto* or *Up* or *The Incredibles*.

I hadn't told Doug when I received my bumper stickers in the mail, hadn't told him when I plastered over 400 of them on cars and mailboxes and bus stop shelters. If he'd noticed them about town, he hadn't said anything. I realized I'd never be able to place all 2000 of them on my own, but I still wasn't willing to tell him or anyone else about them yet.

"Some people would look at you and Toby and think you're so close to the end, why bother splitting." There was no judgment in his tone. I wish I knew how he did that.

"I don't know that we *will* split up," I said. "I just know things can't stay the same."

Perhaps I needed to break things with both Doug and Jonah, too, only go to adult theaters or bathhouses for sex, with no chance of getting dragged into the personal lives…and personal problems…of others.

Doug laughed again, a calming sound, before pulling me close and giving me a deep kiss. "It's *important* to make the most of whatever time we have."

"Even this close to the end, you mean?" I gave him a look of mock outrage.

"Now, now. I understand you old people get sensitive about your age."

"I understand young folks don't know how to treat their elders with respect."

Doug looked at his watch. "My date won't be here for another thirty minutes."

Oh, and I was taking up his time with mediocre banter while he needed to get ready. "I—"

He reached past my belt and underneath the elastic band of my underwear. "Lot of room in here," he said. "You lose more weight?"

I was down to 180. Well, 182 some days and 180 on others. But I kept telling myself I was at 180.

Doug pushed me over the edge of the sofa, pulled my pants down, grabbed some lube, and slowly entered me, a few millimeters at a time. He didn't even really fuck me until another five minutes had passed. I felt like singing along with Carly Simon.

"Anticipation…"

How Doug could stay hard without moving was "Damned impressive," I said.

"Looking at my dick in your ass is stimulation enough."

He began slowly pumping away.

"Unh."

"You okay?"

"Unh. Yeah." I grunted again. Getting fucked was always a little more uncomfortable than I remembered it. Afterward, though, my memories of it were always wonderful.

Like a mother forgetting the pain of childbirth.

Well, perhaps it wasn't a perfect analogy.

I sure didn't forget the pain of my mother telling me never to speak to her again.

"The far right thinks there's a plague of homosexuality," Doug said, a drop of sweat falling onto my back, and I wondered if he was somehow able to read my mind like

Jonah seemed to. People had always said they could read my face quite easily. But these guys were even great at reading the back of my head. "That there are more gays than ever."

"You're not the greatest at sex talk, you know."

Doug gave me an extra hard thrust. "Maybe they're right," he said. "Maybe humans are instinctively trying to slow down procreation, knowing subconsciously on a species level there's no viable future."

"Jesus Christ, Doug."

Doug began pumping even harder, and I could tell from his breathing he was getting close. It still hurt but felt good at the same time. I waited until he was only seconds away before giving him some dirty talk of my own.

"Let's blackmail a right-wing preacher into ordering his congregation to fight climate change!"

Doug shouted as he came and then slumped across my back, laughing. "It's a shame we'll all be dead soon. You'd have been fun to spend a few decades with."

I'd been mortified the first time my doctor told me I was morbidly obese. I supposed I was also morbidly morbid. But gallows humor was still humor. Toby and I had joked sometimes during sex, too, back when we had sex.

Perhaps that's why we stopped having sex.

I didn't want to stop seeing Doug.

There was a knock at the door. "My date's here," Doug announced. He grabbed his pants and headed for the bathroom. "Let her in while I clean up."

Her?

I pulled my own pants up and then walked slowly to open the door. "Hey, Shawna," I said. "What a pretty shirt." A teal that matched her hair.

"Thanks." She looked uncertain, but I ushered her into the apartment. She'd painted her lips the color of coral. "Doug'll be out in a second. Don't mind me. I'll sit out on the balcony and read a book."

Doug soon joined us. We all chatted a few minutes about the latest news, an explosion at an oil refinery in Louisiana, an oil train derailment in Ohio, and a burst pipeline in Michigan. "I have it on good authority," Doug informed us, "that two of those weren't accidents."

Shawna smiled but I didn't. "But…but think of the pollution," I said, "the toxins, the damage to the environment."

Doug shook his head. "The environment can recover faster than the climate. We need to do everything in our power to make life costly and miserable for anyone profiting from fossil fuels."

Shawna shrugged. "There's always friendly fire during war. Collateral damage."

They were talking about *lives*. People with families, with hobbies and dreams and plans. And fish and otters and frogs, that all wanted to fuck and eat, like I did. Birds, too, that just wanted to live out their lives like Toby.

Birds had survived the last mass extinction event, the sole surviving lineage of dinosaurs.

I looked at Doug and Shawna, who were looking back at me. We were undeniably disturbed. Perhaps there was no mass homosexuality as a response to the climate crisis, but there sure seemed to be mass hysteria, collective insanity. That might explain MAGA as much as it explained us.

Doug gave me a kiss and then led Shawna to the bedroom. I got a glass of water and then went to sit on the balcony.

It was too hot.

I came back inside and sat on the sofa, not in the mood to read or watch TV or listen to music. I should probably just go back home to Toby.

I heard the bedroom door open and turned to see Doug beckoning. "Want to watch?" he asked. "And maybe lick my cum out of Shawna's pussy?"

Lord have mercy.

I wasn't the least bit bisexual—I'd even said no to Maggie once during our Human Sexuality course—but no one in their right mind would turn down a chance to lick up Doug's cum. I nodded and joined them in the bedroom.

Ghosts

I had to go back home after work the next day. Staying away any longer would have created a breach too difficult to overcome. But it was impossible to have a normal evening.

It might never be possible again.

"You better not talk about climate tonight," Toby warned. "Why do you have to obsess about it? Are you developing dementia?"

So much for not talking about it.

He had a point, of course. But it was kind of like getting in an accident and bumping my head. Like having a near death experience and then waking up and suddenly being able to see ghosts, if such a thing existed, or people in another dimension.

I remembered the Australian show *Spirited.*

Seeing these other people everywhere and never being able to turn that special vision off would make it impossible to live normally. You could be having a romantic dinner in a restaurant when a ghost started talking to you. Or be in the middle of sex when a ghost started critiquing your performance. Perhaps you were waiting on a customer at work when a ghost started asking questions and speaking over your customer.

You'd never be able to go about life as you had before. It just wouldn't be possible.

Once you could see the stark reality of climate breakdown, you couldn't unsee it. The ghosts were everywhere.

But who in their right mind would want to be partnered to someone who saw ghosts?

"How about I order some teriyaki," I said, "and then we watch a comedy?"

"Sure."

I swallowed four extra fiber capsules to make up at least a little for the additional carbs, but I simply had to accept that my numbers would be out of whack for the evening. Sometimes, you had to sacrifice something good for something that was better.

Toby pulled a blanket over himself as we sat down to watch another episode of the Australian show *Preppers*. I'd turned the AC off so we could hear the television, but we still needed the fan. It made too much noise, too, so I just tried to bear the heat.

"My butt's cold," Toby said.

How could that possibly be, I wondered. Was he sick? We were getting to that age when either one of us could keel over at any moment, not ancient but old enough that no one would be surprised. Even if we were no longer suited to each other, I didn't wish him ill.

"You know what they say, cold butt…"

"You have *never* heard anyone say that in your entire life." Toby tried to sound severe, but I thought I saw a tiny smile.

"Sayings have to start somewhere."

He held my hand while we watched the aboriginal preppers get trapped in their underground shelter.

He fell asleep before the best part.

***

I stood at the bus stop at Mount Baker Transit Center, looking at the back of the bank, where an elderly white man slept underneath a dirty blanket and umbrella. He'd need the umbrella later to protect him from the sun. We hadn't had any rain in weeks.

A tiny Asian woman stood near me, beside the trash can next to the bus shelter.

A young black man, probably in his late twenties, walked over from Rainier, holding up his pants and humming lightly. "It's a great day!" he announced. The Asian woman studied the sidewalk in front of her. "A wonderful day!" the man continued, looking at me.

He had the slim face of an East African immigrant but just the trace of an accent. Perhaps he'd arrived as a young child.

"I used to be homeless," the man said, still looking at me. "But now I have a housing voucher and I'm getting a job."

I nodded in support, but I didn't particularly want to engage.

"I was in prison seven months," he went on, "but I only smoke weed."

Bully for you.

"There's no excuse for being homeless." He looked over toward the man sleeping next to the bank. "People blame everyone else, but there's *no excuse*."

He looked back at me, and now I didn't know what to do. I hardly thought the drastic rise in homelessness the past few years was a result of folks caught up in following the latest trend.

"Don't you agree?" the man pressed.

"I don't know." I desperately wanted the bus to arrive. I had a long day at the drugstore ahead of me and didn't want to arrive already tired from interacting with "the public."

The man shook his head. "The rules suck," he said. "But you have to find a way to make life work." He turned to look at another white man, about forty, who'd just walked up to the bus stop. The white guy acted as if he didn't even see the black man, looking almost in his direction but past him as if there was nothing in that area to notice.

"Don't kick against the pricks," the black man said before walking over to the bus bench and sitting down.

The Asian woman continued studying the sidewalk. The white man pulled out his cell and began chatting energetically with a friend. He wasn't blind so he'd certainly seen the black man but might have already forgotten him. I wasn't sure he'd noticed the white homeless man next to the bank at all.

The guy wore a pressed, button-down shirt and pressed slacks. His leather shoes had been recently polished. His hair was cut close on the left, with a longer wave combed over to the right. Perhaps forty wasn't all that young, but he still looked hip and happening to me.

Mostly, though, he looked *unaware* of anyone besides himself. He chatted now about plans to attend a concert this weekend at the stadium.

Perhaps the only way to live a happy, interesting life was by refusing to see things which might impede that happiness. And wasn't it *good* to enjoy one's life? Whether life was a gift from God or a biological accident, it was ours for only a brief period. Not taking advantage of it would be like having a beautiful dick and choosing celibacy.

The man laughed into his phone again, and I watched the homeless man next to the bank stir.

What must it be like, I wondered, to be born without the empathy gene. Was it a handicap or an incredible stroke of luck?

While I didn't know the answer, I also knew the man chatting happily on the phone would never worry about such a question, because he'd need to have the empathy gene in the first place to be able to ask it.

***

I sat on the sofa, watching the opening credits for *Snakes on a Plane*. I heard a couple of squeaks and looked toward the kitchen. Jonah pushed a cart across the flat carpet in my direction. “Coffee?” he asked. “Tea?” He grinned. “Me?”

Jonah wasn’t old enough to remember that TV movie from the early 1970s starring Karen Valentine, but I was.

“I’ve also got pretzels.” He showed me a tiny blue package. “No more peanuts. Someone might have an allergy.”

“I’m good,” I said. The semaglutide drastically slowed down my digestion, so I wasn’t ravenous most of the time the way I used to be. I still needed to consciously choose not to eat, but at least I could do that now.

“Nothing? Really?” Jonah looked toward the television and then back at me. “Ah, I think I know what you need.”

What I needed was some down time to relax. Watch a fun movie about terrorists on an airplane.

Jonah disappeared into his bedroom and I focused on the start of the story. He returned a moment later with a piece of paper, and I put the movie on Pause.

I took the paper from Jonah and read. He’d printed out a news article from the internet. Apparently, a hacker or hoaxer had tricked Wall Street brokers to dump stock in a company that supplied materials for pipelines and had then bought up most of the stock at pennies on the dollar. She and her friends had managed over the course of a few days to purchase 52% of the shares and then announced they were forcing the company to cancel supplying all fossil fuel projects.

"How did I not hear about this?" I asked, wondering if this was a joke. Satire perhaps? Didn't look like *The Onion*, though. Or Andy Borowitz.

"Maybe mainstream media doesn't want to cover it." Jonah shrugged. "Though they covered the GameStop story and the guy who sent a false Tweet about insulin prices that cratered drug company stocks within minutes."

"Won't some other company just start making money now by becoming the new pipeline supplier?" I asked.

"Hey, you're supposed to celebrate this kind of thing. One victory at a time. You can't win the war overnight."

Jonah sat in my lap, sitting sideways so he could turn one way to see the TV and the other way to look at me. I wrapped my arms around him. He felt good there, but I still wanted to watch the movie. I supposed I was more of a fuddy duddy than I thought.

Oliver Sacks in the conservatory.

"I know what you're thinking," Jonah said.

"Yeah?"

"That I'm *against* this kind of thing." He waved the paper in the air.

"Well…"

Jonah leaned down to kiss my forehead. "I'll have you know that while I was in Dallas, I bought a couple of cans of motor oil and poured them onto Energy Plaza."

I almost laughed at the futility of such an act. Two cans of oil poured on the ground in a city of what...380 square miles? It sounded utterly preposterous. "Why?" Why was it so easy to see what couldn't possibly work only when other people did it?

"One of the flight attendants told me she's retiring," Jonah said. "Too tired of crazy passengers. Everything's a battle these days."

I thought about the woman we'd caught shoplifting condoms, who claimed she was on a mission from God to eliminate birth control.

"Zina didn't sound like she'd have much more fun retired than she had while working." Jonah ground himself a bit more into my crotch. He was blocking the TV screen.

"It struck me that one day, I'll be your age, and I want to at least have a chance at enjoying retirement."

"I can leave you my cane and walker in my will," I offered.

He gave me a look. "Aren't you enjoying your evening?"

"Maybe if you let me unzip."

"It's easy for young people to think we'll never get old. But hanging out with you has made me rethink some things."

"I am *not* going to be able to concentrate on the movie if you keep playing with my nipple ring."

"You say that like it's a bad thing."

Jonah stood and offered me his hand. When I took it, he led me to the bedroom. As I undressed, he pointed to the bedside table, which was another rolling cart. I'd never even noticed before. "Can I offer you a strawberry flavored lube?" he asked. "Watermelon flavored?" He pointed. "We have nipple clamps and poppers…"

"Take your clothes off already."

Jonah smiled. "I think I know what you want."

It wasn't rocket science.

He pushed me onto the bed. "Expect a little turbulence."

Oh, brother. This guy was really a bit much, but I was not going to look a dick gift in the mouth.

Storms

The mercenary leader of the Wagner group was killed in a plane crash in Russia, just months after a failed coup to take down Putin. Ukrainian drones were reaching Moscow more often and setting off explosions in office high rises, but Russian troops were still exacting a higher toll on Ukrainian civilians.

India successfully landed a spacecraft on the moon.

New Orleans experienced eight days of record high temperatures in a row.

Though it was winter in the southern hemisphere, the temperature reached 100 degrees in Argentina and Paraguay, 104 in parts of Chile.

A convicted January 6 terrorist on house arrest ran off while awaiting sentencing.

UPS workers threatened to strike over multiple issues with the company, including the need for air conditioners in delivery vans.

People in France were still protesting Macron single-handedly raising the retirement age, overriding the parliament.

The bodies of eighteen immigrants were found on the Greek border with Turkey after a wildfire tore through the region. The following day, bodies of two more immigrants were discovered.

Hospital patients in a Greek clinic were evacuated by ferry as flames reached the shore behind them.

According to a newly published travel guide, speed skating on the frozen canals of Amsterdam appeared to be a thing of the past, as the canals had only frozen three times in the past ten years.

Kyrgyzstan officials declared a national emergency because of heavy flooding.

Self-Defense Is a Human Right

The rally was being held at five different sites across the city simultaneously. We'd piggybacked onto it and the only thing folks from Movie Night needed to do was put in requests at work early enough to get the day off.

Folks who'd RSVP'd with Greenpeace went to one location while those who'd signed up through the Sierra Club or Nature Conservancy or Earthjustice or Climate Defiance or another organization were asked to gather at other sites. With so many climate or environmental organizations out there, and with several labor and human rights organizations urging their members to join the protest at one of the five sites, too, expectations were high.

That at least there'd be news coverage. Little expectation anyone in power would care enough to change their policies.

"So it's all just for show?" I asked.

"Theater is important," Doug said. "Preaching to the choir is important, too."

"It just feels…"

"Like we should be blowing up pipelines instead?" Doug grinned.

Damned if you do and damned if you don't.

"Let's just go out and have a good time," Doug insisted. "We'll be at Westlake. And then you said you'd be meeting up with Jonah at the City Hall protest?"

I nodded, though really I'd be joining Jonah at the Federal Building on 2nd. I simply didn't want Doug to know any more details about Jonah than necessary. Around Doug, even public actions felt like secrets to be guarded.

Doug asked a lot of questions about Jonah, and I knew he wasn't only thinking about sex because he already had more than enough. Doug had that unidentifiable charisma making it easy for him to get both men and women into bed.

Pheromones? Confidence?

What would the world be like if instead of obsessing over money or power or even sex, more folks nonchalantly engaged in sex with one another without the moral or other judgmental resistance most of us put up every day?

"He's too short."

"He's bald."

"I don't like his nose."

"Ugly lips."

"Too fat."

"Too skinny."

So many reasons to turn away intimacy of any kind that had nothing to do with money or politics, which in turn only added dozens more reasons to feel disgust for one another.

I looked at Doug as he ran his fingers through his sandy blond hair, trying to resist pulling his hand to my face and inhaling deeply. If he could get sex so easily, and he still spent this much time with me, he must actually *like* me.

For Toby's birthday last week, Doug had suggested I pay for an erotic photoshoot for Toby and Martin. It cost way more than we usually spent on each other, and it felt awkward given the tension in our relationship, but Doug got me a discount by fucking the photographer, and it turned out that Toby seemed genuinely touched, if confused.

Doug didn't *have* to help me with Toby, yet he did.

I grabbed my sign, with "What have you got against a stable climate?" on one side and "Global warming will create half a billion immigrants" on the other. I hoped that second thought might give conservatives something to consider.

Of course, capitalism was creating most of the immigration crises around the world now, and no one was doing much about that. Or about any of the other reasons contributing to the problem.

Once on light rail, Doug positioned his sign—"Self-Defense Isn't a Crime" on one side and "Even Santa Knows Coal Is Bad" on the reverse—so that other riders could read the messages. I noticed one tourist frown and take a picture with his phone.

Most passengers ignored us. There were two homeless people in our car and a woman with a yippy dog. Lots of folks to avoid.

But there were two other protesters in our car, too, with their own signs, and when we deboarded at Westlake, we saw two dozen more getting off the other cars. I instantly felt more energized as we climbed the stairs to street level.

Hundreds were already gathered on the plaza and along the sidewalks. Doug wanted a spot right near the platform so he could hear the speakers. He wore his mask and wasn't worried about being seen. I'd have preferred lingering on the edge. But I felt a bit of proxy courage hanging out with Doug these past few weeks, even while feeling plenty of firsthand terror.

It was a total coincidence that the Air Quality Index today was 132, the result of some wildfires out toward Spokane.

Well, I supposed it wasn't really a coincidence but inevitable. At least it kept the temperature in the mid-80s.

We joined other folks from our Climate Movie Night group, Shawna, Sarosh, and Carla. Carla was the woman I thought might be trans. I still couldn't quite be sure. And it irritated me that I kept trying to figure it out.

Doug gave Shawna a kiss, and she gave me a wink. She took quick photos of all of us. I noticed that Doug made sure to pull his mask back up first.

Many protesters wore green. Others wore black plastic garbage bags with the words "Oil is trash" plastered across them. And most people carried signs. Lots and lots of signs.

There Is No Planet B

Ready for Drought and Famine?

Energy Cleanliness Is Next to Godliness

Don't Be Silent at a Time Like This

The Ocean Is Rising And So Are We!

Some canned music, mostly rap and hip hop—though to be honest, I didn't fully understand the difference—played as organizers at Westlake set up. This was always the hardest part of any protest for me. By the time everything got going, almost always twenty minutes late, I was usually ready to head home. But with Doug beside me, that wasn't an option.

He waved at some people in the crowd but didn't introduce me. I saw Rorik, one of the regulars at the drugstore. His head was nearly shaved, with tattooed leopard spots on his scalp visible beneath the green buzz cut. I waved and he waved back.

Thankfully, someone came to the microphone at just ten minutes past 11:00. He offered a land acknowledgement, not worth much but better than not acknowledging indigenous people at all, I supposed. Then he gave a rundown of the latest climate news.

"I'm sure you've heard," he said, "that a climate researcher admitted publicly he falsified data to make it look like climate change was more of a factor in California wildfires than it really was."

I looked at Doug, whose brows furrowed. He turned to Sarosh to say something, but the crowd was so noisy I couldn't hear their conversation.

"It turns out the researcher works for a group that promotes climate misinformation to give deniers the 'proof' they need to keep denying. He wasn't falsifying data to make climate change look worse than it is. He was doing it to undermine the public's confidence in all climate research."

The speaker went on to talk briefly about the tried-and-true methods of the fossil fuel industry to sow doubt but said their latest strategy included pitting climate organizations against each other, trying to get us arguing over whether eating vegan was "the answer" or if banning air travel was.

"They want us to worry about plastic straws, not new drilling."

Doug turned to talk to Shawna, who said something that made him laugh.

I heard a sharp pop and looked around, but it wasn't followed by any more pops, and no one else seemed to have noticed.

A man wearing a black ski mask made his way through the crowd. In this heat, that didn't bode well. It was hard to make out with all the people between us, but it didn't look like he was carrying anything suspicious.

I tried to note where uniformed officers were in case someone started trouble.

I noticed Sarosh holding Carla's hand.

Someone waved a rainbow flag but instead of a pink triangle in the upper left corner, it featured a green triangle.

I saw a woman who looked an awful lot like Maggie.

A couple of other speakers followed the plastic straw guy, some leading chants and others talking about "next steps."

Doug groaned. "They want us to call our representatives again." He grimaced. "As if we haven't done that two hundred times already." He looked away from the speaker and toward me. "Do you remember Einstein's definition of insanity?"

Having the same conversation about next steps over and over and expecting it to end differently?

"We need to dox every fossil fuel executive. Every insurance executive whose company still insures fossil fuel projects. Every senator and representative who votes to subsidize fossil fuels."

"And then what?" I asked. "Send them hate mail?"

Doug looked at me without replying, and I felt a chill, even on this hot summer day.

"Do you know what swatting is?"

I remembered a documentary that suggested Neanderthals went extinct because they weren't as ruthless as *Homo sapiens*.

I wanted to be a *Homo sensorium*. Have group sex with Lito and Wolfgang and all the others in their *Sense8* cluster.

A clusterfuck.

If only humans could go extinct without bringing ten million other species down with us.

"I wish I could distribute a flyer asking folks with relatives who work as oil execs or attorneys for fossil fuel companies to poison them at Thanksgiving."

"Dear sweet Jesus!"

"Do whatever they can. There's no way we can get close to most of these creeps. We need insiders. Thousands of them." He said something to Shawna and then turned back to me. "We need these folks to jump out of windows the way Putin's critics seem to."

I looked at my watch. "I'm going to head over to City Hall," I said. "Talk to you later."

Doug's look was quite cool. He didn't say goodbye. Shawna waved.

It didn't take long to reach the Federal Building. Even in this high-end business district, homeless people lounged about on almost every corner. Downtown Seattle used to feel vibrant. I never came down anymore to stroll through Pike Place Market or see a movie. We didn't come to visit the Aquarium or walk along the waterfront. These all used to be things locals did as often as tourists.

Society was going to be transformed one way or another, whether we liked it or not.

As I approached the Federal Building, I started reading more protest signs. Some people drew images to go along with their slogans. I would have been lucky just to make my letters legible. But I'd printed the words this time to paste onto my sign. While wearing gloves so the tape didn't capture my fingerprints.

We Can't Drink Oil

Don't Be a Fossil Fool

The Climate Is Changing—Why Aren't We?

Don't Burn My Future

Record Oil Profits=Record High Temperatures

Burn Capitalism, Not Oil

Church Leaders—Call Out the Sin of Oil Subsidies

I circled the edge of the crowd, looking for Jonah. It took me ten minutes. He was wearing fatigues, but instead of the traditional olives or tans, his camouflage was made of rainbow colors.

I supposed so he could go into a gay bar and blend in without being noticed.

Of course, I'd had a hard time finding him even among a mostly straight crowd. He put his sign down and hugged me, planting a big, dramatic kiss on my lips before I pulled my mask back up.

I felt inspired and intimidated by Doug. Around Jonah, I felt a comfortable thrill. The problem was that I kind of liked *all* of that.

A black woman spoke to the crowd. I wasn't sure what group she was with. She might have been a candidate for city council. "I was speaking to my ex-husband the other day," she said. "When I told him I was coming to the rally to demand immediate action, he said what you and I have heard a million times already: 'I don't know. I think we need more study.'"

The crowd booed.

"And I said, '*You* may not know, but lots of other people *do*. There are thousands of studies and reports with definitive answers. You're free to catch up to the rest of us, but we're not obligated to wait for you before we act.'"

Now the crowd cheered.

"You can see why we divorced," she added with a grin.

The crowd laughed, but I didn't think that was funny at all.

Another speaker came up after her, an Asian man. He spoke about pushing the Department of Justice to go after Big Oil, for climate activists to attack through as many court cases as possible.

Finally, around 12:45, someone else came up and issued directions for the march. Protesters at all five locations downtown were to converge in front of the bank where we'd held the anti-loan protest a few weeks ago and make one final show there before breaking up for the day.

I'd seen several hundred people at Westlake and a slightly smaller crowd in front of the Federal Building, but by the time we reached the bank, I realized that there must be at least four or five thousand protesters altogether.

I Don't Like Baked Alaska

Oil Kills

What Do You Have Against Clean Energy?

Oil Execs Are War Criminals

Stop Making Excuses

Repent! The End of the Holocene Is Here!

I wondered if we should start tagging buildings across the city with these slogans.

I felt my phone vibrate and looked at the screen. Shawna had sent a text. "Why are there only 4000 people here in a city of half a million?"

Doug had borrowed Shawna's phone.

I put my phone away and raised my sign higher. Jonah smiled and squeezed my hand.

And too soon, it was time to go home. I realized this was the first time I'd ever wanted to stay until the end of a rally. I kissed Jonah goodbye, ran into Miguel from Movie Night on my way to the light rail station and waved, and sent Doug a quick text via Shawna. "Talk to you soon."

Even back on Renton Avenue as I walked home from the bus stop, I held my sign high so that drivers could read it before I turned onto my street.

"Saw you guys on the news," Toby said when I went in the house.

"Yeah?"

"They showed a man in a pink tutu, a man dressed as Spiderman, and a woman with eyebrow piercings, a labret, and a forehead piercing like a small metal horn."

I nodded.

"I've been doing some reading," Toby went on. He turned away as if afraid to look me in the eyes. "How would you feel about painting our roof white?"

When he looked back at me, I held out my hand. When he tentatively grasped my fingers, I pulled him over and we hugged as we hadn't in a very long time.

Drought

A mule carrying a buggy full of tourists in the New Orleans French Quarter died of heatstroke. Two of the tourists demanded a refund.

A nursing home in Mississippi was evacuated when its air conditioning system failed. Residents in nearby Jackson had been without a stable supply of water for almost a year.

A wildfire fueled by winds from an offshore hurricane leveled the town of Lahaina in Maui in a matter of hours. Almost the entire town of 12,000 people was burned to the ground.

Before the fire began, electricity was out, internet was out, and cell phone service was out. Many residents weren't aware of the danger until the smoke alarms in their homes started going off and they looked outside to see what was happening.

Two women huddled in their condo's swimming pool as the buildings around them crumbled. Others jumped into the ocean, cowering behind a seawall or swimming away from boats burning in the harbor.

Families perished in their cars, stuck in traffic. Elderly residents unable to run died in their homes.

One man, knowing his neighbor was at work, grabbed the neighbor's kids and got them to safety as dead birds fell to the ground around them.

Survivors recounted hearing people not even a block away screaming as the flames caught up to them.

The body of a teenage boy was found in his home beside his dog.

So far, 97 charred remains had been recovered.

Right-wing pundits insisted on boycotting Bud Light beer after the company sponsored a trans influencer.

Adapt Like There's No Tomorrow

The bus was fairly crowded, so when I saw a homeless man wrapped in a blanket climb aboard, I tensed. The man was surprisingly good looking, in his forties, with dark hair and a three-day beard. His T-shirt demanding "Ask Me About Jesus" was probably more off putting than his housing status. Cleaned up and under different circumstances, his facial features would have had me staring against my better judgment.

He was out of my league, even as an unhoused man. I couldn't imagine what he'd look like if he hadn't lived a hard life.

The bus was stifling. The idea of carrying a blanket everywhere sounded nightmarish, but I supposed he couldn't afford to leave it lying about. The guy started slowly down the aisle. I could see other riders putting their purses or bags on the empty seats next to them and then looking out the window. I was in the last row on the bottom level, opposite the rear doors, just ahead of the steps leading to the elevated rows at the back of the bus.

Keep walking to the elevated section, I urged him in my head. Keep walking. Keep walking.

The man paused just ahead of my row, glancing only briefly at me and then hanging onto the pole near the door.

The bus jostled and he looked back in my direction. I motioned to the seat next to me. The man didn't acknowledge me with his eyes but sat down, pulling his blanket over himself. Some of it lay on my leg.

I thought about cooties.

At this time of the morning, it would take another twenty-five minutes to reach Mount Baker Transit Center. I closed my eyes and tried to zone out.

Not long after, I felt a nudge against my shoulder and looked over toward the homeless fellow. He was nodding off and bumping up against me, trying to wake up but then falling asleep only seconds later and bumping into me again.

I lifted my right arm and gently placed it across the man's shoulders, pulling him toward me. He looked up, alarmed, but then closed his eyes and rested his head on my shoulder.

I'd never have done such a thing if the man wasn't attractive, an unsettling realization. I hated knowing how often I discriminated against people based on their looks. I supposed it was good that for whatever reason, I'd helped at least one person very briefly for a very little bit, but…

Stop analyzing! I ordered myself. *Just do! Act!*

I texted Doug when I got to work. Then I bought a bottle of lice and scabies poison, just in case.

***

"What motivates you?" Doug's tone wasn't challenging, only curious.

"You mean…like in my job?" I needed an income to pay my bills, of course.

Doug shook his head. "Why are you trying to lose weight?"

I was down to 175 pounds. "Well, it's easier to walk now," I said. "It's easier to tie my shoes. I *feel* better." I wanted to be able to reach the exit on a crowded bus without using my stomach to push people out of the way.

"You didn't answer my question."

I knew what he was getting at. "I want to have sex," I admitted. But it wasn't only that. However accepting I might want to be of my body, I could see the way others looked at me. Not just gay men but everyone. Disgust.

Platonic disgust was no fun, either. And I *did* want to have sex again.

"So was it the reward of sex that motivated you or the 'punishment' of *not* having sex unless you acted that did?"

I understood why Toby walked out of the room when things got uncomfortable.

"Look, Craig, different people are motivated by different things. Some are motivated by fear, others by anger, some by hope. That's why there's no one way to talk about climate breakdown."

I knew I was sometimes a gloom and doom kind of guy. More than once, Toby had pointed out my negativity. Yet even with the constant terrible climate news, I did still hope we could change direction. If I didn't believe that, taking even a minor risk would be pointless.

"I don't believe in hope," Doug said. "You know I believe in action."

"Aren't they almost the same thing?"

Doug shook his head again. "People knew about the problems with the cladding on Grenfell Tower. They had time to act. They had reason to act to prevent a tragedy. There was plenty of hope that the problem could be solved." He closed his eyes, and I saw his jaw tighten. "But no one acted until *after* the building burned and killed seventy-two people. *Then* officials started enforcing codes and improving regulations."

I vaguely remembered a news story from a few years earlier.

"The same thing happened with Boeing," he went on, "when they became aware of a problem that brought down one of their 737 MAX planes. They knew about the problem. They had time to act. They had reason to act to prevent a tragedy. But they *didn't* act until a second plane went down killing everyone on board."

Now that story I remembered clearly. Every time I caught the bus to South Park during the year or two the entire fleet of planes was grounded, I passed fields and fields of recalled 737 MAX airplanes.

"But we have climate disasters almost every day," I said. "Why isn't anyone acting yet?"

"Because it's not one company or even one industry that needs to change. It's everything. And rich people are afraid of losing so much as a dollar."

I tried not to groan. Sometimes, this class consciousness stuff could get wearisome.

"Craig." Doug's tone sounded more serious than I'd ever heard him before. My brows furrowed as I looked at him. "The other day I was up in Bellingham buying a hunting knife."

"Why do you need—"

"And I saw a man I recognized as a BP oil exec."

"Jesus Christ! You didn't—"

"I pushed him down some stairs."

Oh my Lord.

"He didn't move, but I didn't stay to find out what happened."

I felt dizzy. Nauseated. I remembered a scene from *The Dead Zone* where Christopher Walken asks his Jewish doctor a question. If he could go back in time to before Hitler rose to power, would he kill him? The doctor replies that as a physician, he's sworn to uphold life. So yes, he'd kill Hitler.

But what Doug had done was wrong. There was no way to justify such a thing.

And now he'd made me an accessory to murder. At the very least, attempted murder.

I turned around and walked out of Doug's apartment without another word, heading straight home. I looked online to read any news about the guy in Bellingham but couldn't find anything. I couldn't count the number of times I'd witnessed an accident or seen the aftermath of a shooting or other incident and then could find no information about it when I looked online. If I didn't know firsthand that something had happened, I'd never have known about the incident at all.

I looked up another website, found the number for the local FBI office, and punched in the numbers on my cell.

"I need to report a murder," I said when a woman answered. I felt the life draining out of me. "A terrorist act."

***

I was in an interrogation room, both like and unlike things I'd seen on TV. Somehow, I'd expected the room to be larger. But I supposed there was something to be said for making a person feel claustrophobic.

I'd told the agent about Doug pushing the guy down the stairs in Bellingham. Of course, that meant I had to confess my part in the tagging and also to being an accessory in the Molotov cocktail bombing. It felt shitty turning in someone I liked, no matter what he'd done. And it felt shitty to know I could have prevented the attack if I'd said something sooner.

It felt shitty knowing that nothing we did or might do mattered, that the forces determined to set the world on fire were so strong that all we could do was damage our souls trying to fight them.

I remembered Eric Bana's tortured face in the movie *Munich* when he makes love to his wife after tracking down the terrorists who killed Israeli athletes at the Olympics.

That's who the homeless guy on the bus had looked like! I'd kept an eye out for him on other bus trips but hadn't spotted him again.

I tried to focus on my predicament.

I didn't say anything to the agents about Jonah. Or Shawna, Miguel, Sarosh, or the others in the Movie Night group.

There was probably no access to semaglutide in prison, but that would be the least of my problems.

Did alpha male prisoners beat up sixty-two-year-old men? Or were we not a threat to their rule? I supposed I'd find out soon enough. I probably wouldn't do a lot of time, but I wasn't sure I was strong enough to survive even a few months.

I supposed I'd find that out soon enough, too.

The interrogator left the room, and I wondered if it had been wise not to ask for an attorney. There just didn't seem to be much point hiding anything.

Well, other than Jonah and Shawna and Miguel and…

The door opened a few minutes later, and the agent led Doug into the room.

Awkward.

Doug sat where the interrogator had earlier, and then the interrogator left. Doug waited until the door was closed before reaching across the table to grasp my hands. "Snitch, huh?" he said with a weak grin.

What was there to say? There were some lines I just couldn't cross. If that made me a winner of the Moral Darwin Awards, then so be it.

"Over the past year I've been working with the FBI," Doug began, "I've turned in two people."

"What?"

"One guy was planning a school shooting."

What the hell was going on?

"He wanted to leave a manifesto saying that with their energy policies, the government had already decided these kids didn't deserve a future, so why pretend now that they're upset over their deaths."

"Jesus."

"Climate activists are supposed to be trying to save kids, not hurt them."

"You're an agent?" I asked, confused.

"An informer. They want me to catch any crazy people out there."

I frowned. Wasn't *Doug* one of the crazy ones? He'd blown up a car, after all. Even if he'd lied about pushing some guy down the stairs in Bellingham, I *knew* he'd lit the Molotov.

"So I say provocative things to other activists and gauge their response."

Didn't that mean he was goading others? Inciting violence? Wasn't that entrapment? And dangerous for the people he provoked without knowing their reaction?

"You're small potatoes," Doug said. "The FBI doesn't need to arrest you. But we do want you to keep our secret and not tell the others. Can you do that?"

And now *not* snitching felt like the bad choice.

"I know you're friends with Jonah and probably some other activists. You don't need to report every little thing, but I know now that if any of them do tell you about some awful action they're planning, you'll report it to us."

"What did the second person you turned in plan to do?" I asked.

Doug shook his head. "Let's just say it was worse than a school shooting."

***

I was pissed with Doug. I was pissed with the FBI. I was pissed with Toby and with myself and the whole world.

I told Toby I thought I might be getting a cold and had better isolate for the evening. I stayed in my office and watched reruns of *The Nanny*.

How could such a stupid show still be fun after all these years?

I ignored a text from Doug.

I replied to Jonah's text. "Saturday night sounds great! See you then." I still couldn't bring myself to type *U* or *nite* or any of the other shorthand normal people used.

I apparently wasn't very good at adapting.

The problem was that none of us, not even the smartest and most flexible, was going to be able to adapt as quickly as necessary if we wanted to survive.

So perhaps the question to answer first was how to speed up evolution.

Tempest

Over 350 new wildfires had broken out in Greece, making this its worst fire season on record. Vineyards, sheep, goats, and chickens burned. And monasteries, homes, and people.

A retired police officer shot up a bar in southern California, killing three people and injuring several others. He was targeting his ex-wife.

100,000 villagers in Pakistan were displaced by heavy floods. 300,000 more were displaced in Somalia and Kenya from the heavy rains.

University students in Uganda protesting the construction of a 900-mile pipeline were beaten and arrested for trying to deliver a petition to Parliament.

A man in Chicago facing eviction shouted, "You protect property, not people!" before opening fire on the two officers who'd come to take him away. Both officers survived. The tenant did not. A suicide note found in the apartment later explained, "My life is over now anyway."

A group of self-proclaimed Nazis demonstrated in Orlando, Florida, chanting, "We are everywhere!"

Four out of five colonies of emperor penguins studied in Antarctica raised *no* surviving chicks last season because the sea ice they were nesting on melted and fell apart before they were old enough to survive the cold water.

A report was released documenting the murders of over 1900 climate activists in the past decade—from hitmen and organized crime but some killed openly by their own governments.

After Iran recorded the highest heat index ever—158 degrees Fahrenheit—the government closed all schools, banks, and government offices for two days because of continued extreme heat.

The Air Thickens

"How can you watch movies like this?" I asked. "Don't they give you the heebie jeebies?"

Jonah nuzzled his head deeper into my crotch as we cuddled on the sofa. "They don't scare me at all," he said. "They show me that even in the worst situations, people find a way to survive."

We were halfway through *Alive*, a film about the Andes plane crash survivors who were forced to eat their dead friends when rescuers never came. I'd read the book decades earlier as a teenager. But I wasn't a flight attendant.

"I've watched *Fate Is the Hunter* and *Crash* and *Miracle Landing* and lots of others." He looked up at me. "The flight attendants are usually the heroes." He batted his eyes. "We're not just pretty faces."

And lovely chest hair.

I supposed watching these movies made sense in an odd way. Wasn't it the same reason I watched so many Holocaust movies? Because I suspected that sooner or later people would be coming for "the gays" and it would be good to have some idea of what to expect, analyze acts of rebellion and resistance, study the ways people survived the unsurvivable.

On the screen now, I watched as three survivors debated which course of action gave them their best chance. One wanted to climb through the mountains and seek help.

Another wanted to wait for someone to find them, though many days had already passed and the official search was likely over.

And the third guy felt too awkward to say what he thought best. “I’ll do whatever you two decide.”

The character Nando was frustrated and yelled at the guy. “It’s your life that’s on the line! One of these plans will save you and the other will get you killed! Doesn’t it matter to you which one we follow?”

I was usually pretty goal oriented, but I took my time fucking Jonah that night, drawing out our lovemaking a full forty minutes.

When I got home, I found Toby asleep, Martin in the bed beside him. This would be at least his fourth sleepover. They’d fallen asleep tonight spooning. It was probably time to start paying more attention to his presence in our lives.

Martin was probably three inches shorter than Toby at maybe 5’ 7” and so slept in front as they spooned. I stood in the bedroom doorway watching, feeling like a parent checking in on his sleeping kids.

I felt happy to see Toby having a good night. I’d be sure to wake up first in the morning and have eggs and veggie sausage ready for them when they came out for breakfast.

***

It had to be done. At some point, I needed to talk to Doug again away from an interrogation room.

"Thanks for coming over." Doug ushered me into his apartment. Once the door was closed, he looked at me expectantly.

I didn't know what to say.

"I'm so glad you reported me." Doug managed a weak smile. "I wanted you to be one of the good guys."

"We committed crimes together," I said. "Felonies."

Doug waved his hand as if swatting at a fly. "Oral sex was a felony in some states until a few years ago, even for married heterosexual couples."

I wanted to be angry but was too tired. "If we just make up the rules as we go and ignore the ones we don't like…"

"What?"

"Aren't we trying to *save* civilization?" I asked. "Civilization requires a shared set of rules."

Doug scrunched up his nose. "I suppose. But don't we already have double standards everywhere? Even triple standards sometimes. And we still have civilization."

A weasel answer.

"Who made the rule," Doug asked, "saying we can't hold people accountable who create climate disasters that kill other people? Who? *Who* made that rule?"

I put both hands on my head like I was holding it in place. "I don't understand. You're reporting people to the FBI who try to do anything drastic. And you've already convinced me that only drastic acts have any chance of making a difference."

Doug took one of my hands and led me to the bedroom.

"Really, Doug?"

As I sat on the bed, he took my phone and went back out to the living room. Then I heard him turn on some music. Back in the bedroom, he closed the door and sat beside me, nuzzling my ear.

I was going to punch him.

Well, no, that would be wrong. But…

"Craig," he whispered, licking my earlobe, "there are things I couldn't say in that interrogation room." He darted his tongue deep into my ear. I shivered.

"Like what?"

Doug reached over and began lightly fingering my nipple ring through my shirt.

"I was recruited because I was already an activist," he whispered, sniffing and nuzzling my neck. He nipped at my shoulder.

Damn those pheromones. They had to be real.

"I thought they were right at first to go after dangerous people, but it didn't take long for me to see that the real danger was in not acting."

Doug untucked my T-shirt and pulled it up over my head. He pushed me gently onto my back and leaned over me, licking first one nipple and then the other.

"I realized that I could use my position to get away with things I could never do before." He stuck his tongue into my navel and wiggled it. Thank God I'd cleaned out the lint a few days earlier.

I put my hands on Doug's head, running my fingers through his thick hair. He moaned.

"I can blow up a car and tell the agents I need to prove myself to extremists so I can find who might be planning to do something worse."

Doug reached for my belt and began unbuckling it. Then he unfastened the button at the top of the waistband and pulled on my zipper. I lifted my butt so he could pull my pants down.

"I got away with shooting out the tires of a fuel truck over in Yakima," he said, licking the head of my dick. He put his face into my pubic hair and inhaled.

"I didn't hear anything about that." I wanted to pull Doug's shirt off, too, but I was still too angry to want to satisfy him. I pulled his head up, positioning his mouth over my dick. He opened up and slowly descended upon me.

Now it was my turn to moan.

"I use my cover," Doug said softly when he came up for air, "to avoid investigation."

"But..." I groaned as he resumed gliding up and down. "...you could still never do anything really impactful without being stopped."

Doug pulled off and grasped my dick with his hands, tugging gently at me. "I can't talk with that thing in my mouth," he said, continuing to stroke.

"What are you hoping to do?" I asked. I couldn't keep my eyes open. The feel of his hand on me forced my eyelids closed.

"Lots of police officers and FBI agents and folks in the military are secretly white supremacists," he said, quickening his rhythm as I dug my ass into the mattress. "It's only natural to assume some of us, even the informers, are secretly pro-human rights."

"Unh."

"I'm going to find enough people here in Seattle to do at least one important action. If I get caught after that, that's okay. I'm going to do *one* thing to hurt fossil fuels."

I remembered Jamie Lee Curtis being interrogated in *True Lies*.

Doug wasn't using lubricant and his spit had dried up, but his grip and rhythm were still working wonders. I could feel my skin burning, knew I was getting chafed, and yet I kept wriggling on the mattress, urging the slight tingling I felt to grow stronger.

"Unh."

"Are you with me, Craig?"

"Oh my God."

He started tugging faster. "Are you with me?"

I groaned loudly as I spurt across my abdomen and stomach, halfway up to my nipples. I hadn't shot that far in decades.

I lay on the bed, breathing heavily and looking into Doug's eyes. I liked this man.

Why were humans so stupid?

Doug ran his finger through part of my cum and slid the tip of his finger into my mouth.

"You care," Doug whispered. "That's the most important part of bravery."

He ran his finger through another part of the line of cum and slid his finger back into my mouth. I licked off my cum again. I could take it in small doses, and when delivered by another man.

"I won't tell you who the others are that I've scoped out," Doug said. "But I'll brainstorm with each of you separately until we come up with a plan."

He ran his finger through yet another part of my cum and let me lick it off again.

"I can tell you, though, that people say a lot of things after sex they might not normally say." He grinned. "It's one of my favorite tools."

I supposed my profile mentioning activism had made me irresistible. As a suspect.

Doug climbed out of bed, ripped his clothes off in seconds, and lay down on top of me, rubbing the rest of my cum against his own chest as he kissed me for the next few minutes. When he finally pulled back, I managed to get in a few words.

"Speaking of favorite tools…"

Doug nodded. He reached over to the bedside table, grabbed a bottle of lotion, and lubed up. As he slid slowly inside me and started drilling, I tried to think up some halfway meaningful way to cripple oil companies that would allow me to use my strengths.

But I wasn't quite sure I had any.

***

It wasn't as if there weren't lots of guys out there looking for sex. It was just that half of them said things like, "I want to be dominated by a man who knows what he wants." I knew what I wanted, and it wasn't to dominate anyone. Many of the other profiles had men saying, "I want to dominate you." That wasn't going to work for me, either.

And the others? An awful lot had age limits, requiring sex partners "under 60." Just missed that cutoff. Still others demanded "fit" or "athletic" men. Good luck there, mister. Even in my prime when I was fit, I wasn't athletic.

I kept casting my net wider, searching first for men within five miles, then six miles, then eight miles, then ten miles.

While online cruising was frustrating, I realized I'd been lucky beyond belief to find two eager fuck buddies already, even if one of them was about to get me put in prison for the rest of my life.

***

"You can't be serious." I held my legs in the air for Jonah as I shook my head.

"I know you want it."

How could he know that? Was he an algorithm? And what in the world had I clicked on to tip him off?

"I saw you looking at it while we had sex last time."

How did he know I was wondering how he knew?

Jonah slid a condom over the cockpit and forward fuselage of his model DC9, lubed it up, and directed the captain and copilot toward my asshole.

"Trouble ahead?" I asked.

Jonah shook his head. "Smooth sailing."

The next several minutes felt pretty turbulent to me. But turbulent in a good way. Even though I didn't shoot as far as I had the other day with Doug, I still impressed myself if not Jonah.

After he shot onto my face a few minutes after that, Jonah scooted down so he could lick my forehead, nose, and lips clean.

Moustaches were lick proof, thank goodness, so I could still smell his cum.

"Why can't we just call in some bomb threats?" he asked. "We could disrupt banks that keep making loans to fossil fuel companies. Or shut down gas stations. Or shut down oil company headquarters. Whatever. Disrupt things for a few hours each time without endangering or hurting anyone."

"We absolutely can," I said. We'd have to use burner phones but that seemed perfectly doable.

It struck me that the same way many political statements we considered routine today but which would have been unacceptable only a few years earlier, forms of protest that even a few months ago would have seemed inappropriate now felt tame.

I remembered watching an interview with a woman who'd been trapped by fire in a high rise in New Orleans. At first, when her friends suggested they try to lower one of the group out the window to the floor below, letting her kick in the window, she'd felt the suggestion too horrible to contemplate. Only a few minutes later, she was willing to do far more and leapt out the window, landing in a broken heap on the pavement below, the only one of her friends to survive.

"Excellent!" Jonah hopped out of bed and tossed me my boxer briefs. "Now that that's settled, let's watch a movie." He pulled on a pair of sweats. "Have you seen *Catch Me If You Can*?"

Sparks

A Category 4 hurricane weakened to a tropical storm before striking California but still caused widespread flooding. A friend of Toby's in Palm Springs hosted a hurricane party.

Thousands of schools across the country were preparing to start the school year without adequate—or sometimes any—air conditioning.

Over a thousand wildfires burned across Canada, most of them out of control. Already the fires had burned more than double the previous annual record number of acres. Yellowknife in the Northwest Territories evacuated almost all of its 20,000 residents on the one road leading out of town.

Upset about Trump's latest indictment, Matt Gaetz of Florida called for violence and "brute force" as the "only way" to clean up Washington.

Sarah Palin insisted people needed to "rise up."

Trump's glowering mug shot sparked memes comparing him to Malcolm McDowell in *A Clockwork Orange* and Jack Nicholson in *The Shining*.

Ten billion snow crabs were missing from the Bering Sea off Alaska, devastating a $200 million a year industry, the decline almost certainly caused by loss of sea ice, essential for the survival of young crabs.

New Orleanians were warned that drought was causing salt water to creep up from the Gulf and that drinking water might soon be impacted. Frightened residents rushed to the store and bought up almost the entire supply of bottled water within hours.

Desperate Times

"What do we need?" the woman with the megaphone shouted.

"Desperate measures!" the crowd shouted back.

"Why do we need them?" the woman shouted again.

"Desperate times!" the crowd shouted as they waved their signs.

Toby and I watched the short news segment about a climate protest in Houston. Police rushed in and started firing rubber bullets. Two protesters lost teeth. One reporter lost an eye.

"Okay," Toby said. "Let's get it over with."

"What?"

"We're going to have our obligatory climate talk now, aren't we?" He sighed.

I was simultaneously amused and irritated.

"All right," I agreed. "We need a global Nuremberg Trial for those who do things that have destroyed the stability of our climate. Internal documents at several fossil fuel companies prove they *knew* there'd be 'catastrophic' results from continued oil production. They even realized it would be a threat to the survival of civilization itself."

"If you say so."

I looked at him.

"You're a lot of work, Craig, and I retired because I don't want to keep working."

And I thought that limp dick comment had cut me to the core.

"Everything's a morality test with you. And no matter which morality test you give me, I always fail because there's no way to win them. They're all Kobayashi Maru morality tests."

"But they're not *War Games* morality tests," I said. "This isn't Joshua the computer saying 'The only way to win is not to play.' *Not* playing is the one sure way to lose."

"I'm seventy years old, Craig."

"And both your parents lived into their nineties."

Toby groaned. "I don't want to be in a relationship where it'll be a relief when my partner dies."

Jesus Christ. And I thought the "You're a lot of work" comment had cut me to the core.

"We want different things." Toby looked at me with the saddest eyes I'd ever seen.

Now I was the one to sigh. "Why don't you call Martin and invite him over for dinner?" I asked. "I'll order you guys a pizza, and I'll drink a protein shake in my office so you can have the living room to watch something."

"Oh, Craig."

I put my hand on his shoulder. “It’s okay, Toby.” I kissed him on the cheek. “You should have something you want tonight. And this is as close as I can come to giving you that.”

He pulled me into a weak hug. “I wish things were different,” he whispered.

I did, too.

***

“Not another airplane disaster, please,” I begged.

“It’s only forty-five minutes.” Jonah clasped his hands together as if praying. In addition to his airplane movies, he also watched the series *Mayday: Air Disaster*, which featured different crashes or near crashes from airlines all over the world. “This episode is about an Air France flight that crashed in Toronto during turbulence.”

Toby’s friends Clayton and Ben were finally relocating to France in two weeks.

“Okay,” I said, “but then I want forty-five minutes of bedroom time after.”

“Sounds like a win/win to me.”

Jonah and I cuddled on the loveseat made from airplane seats. High above the clouds, the flight onscreen was calm from Paris to Toronto. Their position made them oblivious to the danger below. But once below the clouds, their world changed instantly.

The plane didn’t even touch down until midway along the runway, and they’d been assigned the shortest runway to begin with because of the wind direction. The copilot was gripping the controls so tightly to fight crosswinds he forgot to deploy reverse thrusters for another thirteen seconds.

And then they reached the end of the runway and crashed down an embankment.

That's when the fire started. "I don't think I can watch." I buried my face in Jonah's shoulder as he continued looking at the screen, riveted. I knew I was listening to actors, but the screams still tore at my chest.

I remembered watching *Sullivan's Travels* as a teen, a Depression-era movie about a filmmaker trying to make "meaningful" films who discovers that suffering people just need a reason to laugh and escape their misery for a few hours at a time.

"Ooh, that makes me mad!"

I looked up to see Jonah glaring at the screen.

"That stupid passenger is slowing everyone down *in a fire* by bringing their damn luggage with them." He growled. "Priorities, people! Priorities!"

I watched as several passengers, covered in mud and dripping wet, clambered up the embankment while the plane behind them burned.

Miraculously, though, all 300+ passengers and crew survived the crash.

Jonah let out a loud sigh as the final credits rolled. "See? That's why I watch these things."

I shook my head. “I don’t know. It’d be like watching a documentary about STIs before coming over to fuck.”

Jonah shrugged. “Probably not a bad idea, to be honest.”

For one anniversary, Maggie had sent me a color atlas of sexually transmitted diseases. Another year, she’d sent an illustrated guide to proper anal douching.

So sweet.

“On that note,” I said, “maybe I should take an extra dick pill before we head to the bedroom.”

***

Toby and I played a short game of Scrabble after dinner. He turned the radio to smooth jazz, which he knew I didn’t like, but he wasn’t being provocative, just trying to make the evening bearable for himself.

“Do you want to live with Martin?” I asked, adding an E and W to Toby’s C-A-S-H.

“Craig, let’s not talk about divorce.”

“We don’t have to divorce, do we? You can still live with him.”

Toby studied his tiles for a long while and finally added an S to “CASHEW” before adding T-A-R going down from the S. “I’m too old for big changes.”

“Even if it would make your life better?” I added a K to Toby’s STAR.

"But we don't know that my living with Martin would make life better. I don't know if I want to take the risk."

"You could ask him to move in temporarily and see how it works. I'm already on the sofa, after all." They seemed to fit well enough. Martin was only fifty-five, his hair still full of color, if you could call ash colorful. It looked good on him, though, even if it was thinning on top. He kept it trimmed short, not trying to hide anything.

I appreciated the frankness.

"You'll feel left out."

"I already feel left out."

Toby looked at the board and added an L-E-Y to my last word.

"That's excellent!" I gave him a thumbs up.

"I'll think about it."

***

I mailed Roger a card congratulating him on buying a home in Bodega Bay, not as far north as he'd hoped to relocate but still peaceful compared to San Francisco, even with the occasional Hitchcock tourist poking about.

***

"Hey, Kaymeena." I'd just come home from work and decided to water the trees and blueberry bushes in the front yard before going inside. Some of the leaves were starting to curl. We'd already lost a small hydrangea to neglect.

Kaymeena stepped out of her car, still looking fresh after a long day at work. "How's Toby?" she asked.

"Good. And Christopher?" I turned off the hose.

"He really likes our new pastor."

"Your youth choir performing again soon?"

Kaymeena and I chatted a few more minutes while I helped her pull bins from the curb to the side of her house. She mentioned she'd gone to Columbia City to pick up some pastries the day before and had seen several businesses with their front windows broken.

"The hamburger place in Mount Baker had its front door bashed in," I said. "The bank, too, right by the transit center."

And no suspects had been caught yet, even for the vandalism at the bank.

What did it say about me that I found the lack of arrests a good sign?

"The world's becoming so wicked." Kaymeena shook her head. "I can't wait until the Second Coming." She fingered the cross around her neck absentmindedly.

I waved goodbye then and went inside, where I found Toby doing something wicked to Martin.

I grabbed some vanilla yogurt out of the freezer.

At least they let me watch.

***

I met Doug at Seward Park, afraid to go to his apartment again. Maybe with an outdoor breeze, I wouldn't be as susceptible to his pheromones. Or my irrational belief they were the cause of my irrational lust.

"This isn't something to endure for a few months," he said, "while waiting for things to return to normal."

"What do you want from me?"

"The climate will keep deteriorating long past the time we finally take action, if we ever do. You can't stop a 100-car freight train in two seconds."

I remembered a report about mile-long freight trains with only one conductor aboard, no one at the rear any longer to help. "You want to blow up a freight train?"

"Craig, you grew up expecting a certain kind of life. At least expecting that a certain kind of life was *possible* if you worked hard and were very lucky." He held my hand as we made the loop around the former island.

"I came out in the middle of the AIDS epidemic," I reminded him. "With Reagan as president and Thatcher as prime minister."

"I grew up with 9/11 and *An Inconvenient Truth*."

Sometimes, I still felt thirty years old, and other times, I felt a hundred. At sixty-two, I'd lived long enough that just four of my lifetimes—four!—would bring us back to 1775, before the Declaration of Independence had even been signed.

"I grew up trying not to think about the future," Doug continued. "Why plan for retirement when you don't believe politicians will even allow the program to exist by the time you reach your sixties?" Doug stopped as we reached the part of the path where we could look out toward Mercer Island. Probably the most expensive real estate in the area, the richest of the rich surrounding themselves with a moat made of Lake Washington.

"Why plan for retirement," Doug went on, "when you don't think humans will even be around anymore?"

"You don't really think we'll go extinct, do you?"

He shrugged. "I just know I'd rather die than be a prepper and try to survive the mess that's coming."

I thought about aborigines.

"So why be an activist at all?" I felt I'd asked the same question a dozen different ways. It was like a cancer patient continuing to ask, "Why me?" over and over.

"Because I don't *know* that scientists won't develop some kind of carbon capture. I don't *know* that a new virus won't kill off 40% of the human population, giving the rest of us time to change our ways." He turned to face me. He looked a bit scruffy today. I wasn't sure he'd bathed this morning. Even outside, I could smell his body odor faintly. *Not* pheromones, to be sure. "It's probably in our DNA to hope when we shouldn't."

I was so very tired of hoping. For friendships, better health, a decent job…

I was still at 175 pounds. I'd finally hit the plateau I'd heard so much about. I had at least another twenty pounds to lose and might not ever lose them.

I wasn't sure it was worth trying to increase the dose I was injecting. I'd read recently of people developing stomach paralysis or other unexpected side effects.

I remembered a scene from *Jurassic Park* when the scientists pointed out that when you created something new in the world, you couldn't possibly hope to control it. You could never really know what to expect.

It had to be true of carbon capture, too. Or whatever new forms of energy we tried to harness. Whatever good they brought us, they were sure to bring some unexpected bad effects, too. It was simply that, like my weight, we were at a point where we had no choice but to try. I either needed the very expensive semaglutide, the more expensive tirzepatide, or a gastric bypass.

Whatever the side effects, the problems that came with doing nothing were unsustainable.

"Can you come over tonight after 8:00?" I asked.

"Really? Your place?"

"Toby's boyfriend is spending the night and I thought maybe you should, too."

"Hmmm."

"I think we need to start looking at *everything* differently from now on."

***

Things were tense at times, especially when Martin seemed to ogle Doug a bit too long, a bit too often. But we all chatted for an hour while listening to music, and when Toby and Martin retired to the bedroom, I led Doug downstairs to the basement.

"We haven't used the sling in a few years," I said. "But you're right about hope. I couldn't bear to part with it, just in case."

"Oh, I'm the case!" Doug grinned. "And you better not say 'nutcase'!"

"Nope, that would be me."

"Help me into this thing," Doug said, shucking his clothes.

"You're going to bottom?"

"Well, I'll be first anyway. You moan more if you've already cum before I fuck you."

I ended up moaning so loudly that Toby and Martin came downstairs to watch. When Doug and I finished, they took over our positions and we watched. Toby had apparently already cum upstairs, so Martin fucked him. With a definitely *not* limp dick.

His slight dad bod paunch slapped up against Toby's ass with a satisfying smack again and again. Sexy as hell.

When they finished, all four of us gave each other quick pecks goodnight, and then Toby and Martin returned to the bedroom while Doug joined me on the sofa. He didn't need to sleep sitting up, so he lay with his head in my lap.

***

For Movie Night, one of the activists brought a DVD of *The Wobblies*. Astounding how little labor history any of us had ever been taught in school.

It wasn't an oversight.

"Everyone always points to France and says, 'They know how to protest,'" Doug said. "But we know how, too. *Anyone* can fight for what's right."

"Are you going to lead from the front or from behind?" Jonah asked, his tone a little too sharp.

Several heads swiveled toward him. He'd already made several snippy comments directed at Doug since the meeting began a couple of hours earlier.

"Someone just attached bombs to fifteen yachts in Galveston," Shawna interjected, probably trying to defuse the tension. "Sank them all and two others that caught fire next to them."

"Anyone know who did it?" asked Miguel.

"Was it a response to the police attacks in Houston?" Sarosh asked.

"I'm happy to lead from in front," Doug said, "if you'll commit to standing behind me."

"What are you planning?" Jonah asked. "You going to blow up gas stations? Bomb some refineries?"

Holy hell.

Jonah's tone now was hard to measure. I couldn't tell if he was being sarcastic or serious, judgmental or hopeful.

"You mean we," Doug said.

Jonah nodded. "Are *we* going to bomb car dealerships so people stop buying cars? Are *we* going to drop firebombs on the homes of oil executives?"

I hadn't said a word to him about Doug buying drones. But it didn't take much browsing through Doug's DVD shelf to understand the possibilities.

Were we all going to be prosecuted for Movie Night racketeering?

"You can't reason with an addict," Doug insisted. "And if the addict has money and power and law behind him, what's left?"

"I just want to watch Eurovision!" Miguel said, following Shawna's attempt to lighten the mood.

"Pretending the war isn't real because it hasn't touched you personally is like the workers at Mitsubishi feeling safe in the summer of 1945."

At least it wasn't a Hitler analogy.

"Just how many innocent people do you plan to kill to end the war?" Jonah asked.

Doug turned to me, and more heads swiveled to watch the exchange. "Don't you sometimes just want to plug that blowhole with a dick?" he asked.

I was the second-to-last person to leave for the evening. Jonah stayed after I headed out. I honestly wondered if either of them would still be alive by morning.

Heat

COVID cases rose across the U.S. Some bus riders in Seattle still wore masks, but most of those wore them on their chins.

Milan had its hottest day in 260 years.

A white man targeted and killed three black shoppers at a Dollar Store in Florida.

Parents of children gunned down in a Christian school in Tennessee were kicked out of a public hearing for peacefully insisting on modest gun regulations.

Right-wing influencers blew up dollhouses after determining that Barbie was too woke.

At least 73 people were killed in Johannesburg when a fire broke out in a five-story building occupied by indigent workers.

Fentanyl deaths in the U.S. topped 77,000, more than the total number of deaths from car accidents and murders combined. Public health officials called many of them "deaths of despair."

Sabotage was suspected when an underwater pipeline between Finland and Estonia suffered damage from "physical force."

Canada issued a U.S. travel advisory, telling its LGBTQ citizens to be careful because of the growing anti-LGBTQ sentiment and legislation here.

A prominent climate scientist predicted that within a few years, heatwaves would no longer be killing thousands of people over the course of a few days but a million.

Many Hands Make Light Work

"I don't want to hurt your feelings," Toby said.

A bit late for that.

"You're just not...well, you're not hot," he said. "I mean, you look good enough, but..."

"Yes?"

"Even at your best, sex was never exciting." Toby shook his head, looking upset with himself for not having the right words. "You're just too casual about it. I like guys who shout and talk dirty and get wild."

"And I'm too laid back."

He shrugged.

Toby wasn't wrong. While internally, I could be enjoying the hell out of a sexual encounter, I realized that one of the things I especially liked was the casual aspect of it. Not dismissive or unappreciative or jaded. I simply wanted to be able to talk about sex—and have sex—the way I might talk about a TV show I really liked. Enthused and engaged without the conversation carrying so much weight I needed to mentally prepare for it as if I were giving a TED talk in front of thousands.

A friendly sexual encounter *to me* was hotter than a "passionate" encounter. The casual sharing of body parts, the casual vulnerability, the casual entering of a space that should be private but which we'd opened to one another the way strangers meeting at church might shake hands.

I remembered a time I stepped onto the elevator at Westlake light rail station and a man in the elevator with me had looked at me questioningly, nodded as if understanding I'd consented, and then groped me before pulling me into a kiss. He never even said a word as the doors opened and he headed on his way.

It was like handing a daisy to someone who looked a little down, a friendly way to cheer someone up.

I *liked* that.

Every encounter didn't need to carry weight.

"Toby, I love you, but no one can be everything for another person." It was one of the reasons I'd insisted on an open relationship from the start. But even that agreement hadn't solved the problem.

He shook his head. "It's not possible." Toby glanced at his phone, though it hadn't pinged.

"And it would be too big a burden even if it were."

"Martin's great," Toby said, "but sometimes…"

I kept quiet.

He grinned shyly. "I guess I do miss the way you used to kneel down and rim me while I washed the dishes."

"Casually."

He nodded.

"I'm glad you've found Martin," I said. "And I'm enjoying both Doug and Jonah's company, even if they aren't too crazy about each other."

Toby looked at his phone again and scrolled, frowning when nothing new seemed to pop up.

"I want both of them," I said. "And I still want you."

Toby finally looked up from his phone.

"I'd like all of us to be friends. And of course, because I like casual sex, I'd like for you to feel you can casually approach Doug and Jonah, too, if you want. Or passionately, for that matter." And if they welcomed either approach.

"I'm not sure how Martin will feel."

"You might want to ask."

That was as much heavy conversation as Toby could handle for one evening, so we sat on the sofa watching a rerun of *The Golden Girls* while holding hands. I got up at one point to cut an apple in half and then set two saucers down on the coffee table.

"The Val St. Lambert looks good in the kitchen nook," I said, biting off a piece of my apple slice.

"You noticed."

After the show was over, Toby went to wash both saucers in the sink.

I knelt on the floor behind him and pulled down his sweats. He leaned forward to finish washing, humming a tune from Pink while I took care of him.

***

"Jonah's weird," Doug said, "but I'm hardly in a position to talk."

"Well, you'll be with Toby tonight in the bedroom while Jonah and I have our way with Martin in the basement."

"And are we friends?" Doug asked. "Fuck buddies? Are all five of us *dating*?"

"I have no idea. We're creating something new. It won't look like what we're used to." Though I expected we weren't the first to try it. These kinds of things simply didn't get a lot of press.

"No climate talk tonight?"

"We've got a delicate ecosystem here and need to take a bit of extra care for now."

He sighed. "Then *tomorrow* you and I are going out to shop for more spray paint."

I shook my head. "No, you and Jonah will go out and shop."

"Aren't you the little matchmaker?" He started humming a tune from *Fiddler on the Roof*.

"No, I'm still a Large," I said. "But l'chaim."

We spent the next several minutes examining each other's most Jewish feature. A circumcised cock tasted pretty good when dipped in chocolate syrup. At least, that's what Doug said. I intended to save my calories for later. I'd brought over some whipped cream.

***

A woman who'd escaped a burning car by running across a burning field near Lahaina finally succumbed to her injuries after weeks in the burn unit.

What kind of god would let that poor woman suffer so long for nothing?

What kind of god let people survive under earthquake rubble for two weeks and then die on their way to the hospital?

If there was a god, why didn't he/she/it care enough about other species to wipe out half the humans on the planet?

No one was going to help us out of this mess besides ourselves.

***

A portly Latino in his thirties fumbled at length with his wallet while purchasing a package of condoms at the drugstore. At first, I thought he didn't have enough money but slowly realized this was his attempt at flirting. Kellyn was on break, so I took a chance and flirted back.

"Are these the right size?" I asked, holding up the package to squint at the front. "We have larger ones in stock."

I peered down toward the man's beltline, which was hidden by the edge of the counter.

The customer froze and I realized I'd gone too far.

"I could always stop by later and make sure they fit properly." In for a penny…

The man glanced around nervously and then quickly pulled out a piece of torn paper with his name and number handwritten on it before he'd come up to the counter.

It turned out he was one of the passionate types who wasn't all that thrilled with my casual approach. The good news was that the condoms were, in fact, too small, and I had to suck him off without them.

***

"It's not forest fires reaching out into private lands," the climate researcher told the interviewer, "it's fires starting on private lands going into forests." A map appeared on the screen. "Most fires start on grasslands or shrublands. They're brush fires." A video clip of burning grass appeared. "While forest management is part of the problem, it's not the biggest part. These fires aren't driven by too much fuel in the forest. They're driven by the wind. The fuel is the houses, not 'too many trees.'" Video of homes burning in a wildfire appeared. "People are building more homes near these shrublands, in wind tunnels." Another map appeared. "Add that to climate change, and we have a perfect recipe for disaster."

Toby knocked on my office door, and I clicked out of YouTube. "Martin wants some alone time with me tonight. You okay with seeing one of your friends?"

"I'll call Jonah."

***

"Doug's got me thinking."

I was on my knees behind Jonah as he washed dishes at the sink. He seemed to like being casually rimmed as well.

"He's annoying that way," I said when I came up for air before heading back in.

"He said we're the new French Resistance." Jonah grunted. "You know you might be executed but you're fighting for something greater than yourself."

I kept working on his asshole.

"You must have the strongest tongue muscle of anyone I know."

"I exercise." I got back to work.

"I've been thinking."

So he'd said.

"I want to get my first tattoo."

I pulled back. "Really? Of what?"

"A green triangle and the word 'Resist!'"

In the camps, green had been used to mark "criminals," but I supposed that still applied.

I needed my tongue for the rest of this conversation, so I stood, pressing up against Jonah's bare ass. "You can't even watch when I inject myself."

"I intend to ask for a very specific reward afterward."

"Is there anything you want I don't already do?"

He leaned back and whispered something in my ear.

"Okay. That's new. But I'm game."

"And *you* get a tattoo at the same time."

"Hey!"

"I found a tattoo parlor in Columbia City. We have an appointment Wednesday evening after you get off work."

"Presumptuous."

Jonah unbuckled my belt and pulled my pants down. "Turn around. I want to get another look at that ass while it's still a blank canvas." He leaned down behind me and touched a spot here and there on both cheeks. "Hmm. *Lots* of room to write."

"You'll pay for that, mister."

"I will," Jonah agreed. "I'm footing the bill for both tattoos."

I couldn't really ask for a different reward. The one he was asking of me already was reward enough.

***

The tattoo artist turned out to be even more presumptuous than Jonah. "You sure you want to have something permanent that will last *the rest of your life*?"

If he hadn't been looking at the gray in my hair while asking, I might have interpreted his words differently.

But you didn't really want to call the man about to stab you a thousand times with a needle "Bitch," so I just nodded.

Jonah went first and made no sound as Roberto worked on his upper arm, though I saw two tears trickle down his face as he gritted his teeth.

When it was my turn and I lay down with my naked butt facing the ceiling, Roberto said, "It takes a little longer when skin loses its elasticity."

I *really* wanted to call him a bitch now.

Jonah held my hand but didn't speak, not wanting to distract the tattoo artist. He listened to Spanish pop music as he worked, and I spent the next hour or so reflecting on my life. I was estranged from my family. I'd studied literature and film in college as electives but ended up a cashier. I'd applied to medical school, even scored well on the MCAT, but during my interview, the dean told me I didn't have the right personality to be a physician.

It felt worse than being turned down for having a limp dick or being unenthusiastic in bed.

But the dean had probably been right. Despite what Toby thought, my strength was my bedside manner.

If only there were a demand for sixty-two-year-old escorts.

And I'd thought fighting for greener energy was a stretch.

“Keep this out of the sun until it heals,” Roberto said, setting his instruments aside.

Oh, I was *not* recommending this guy.

He held a mirror above me and handed Jonah another mirror to hold below my face so I could see the results. “Increase all hope, ye who enter here.” And there were “arrows” on both cheeks pointing toward my asshole, arrows shaped like dicks.

Okay, *maybe* I’d recommend him.

Glimmers

Another report was released showing the rapid depletion of multiple aquifers in the U.S., a problem in other countries, too. Fracking, of course, injected vast amounts of toxic chemicals into the remaining groundwater.

Over 70,000 people were stranded at the Burning Man festival in Nevada after freak rainstorms caused mudslides that blocked roads in the Nevada desert.

Torrential rains in central Spain washed away bridges near Toledo, the new normal for summer showers when a warmer atmosphere was able to hold so much additional water.

Researchers learned that fall colors were becoming slightly less vibrant each year.

Increasing numbers of Americans believed that vaccines gave their dogs autism and so stopped vaccinating their pets even against rabies.

A man at a MAGA rally said on camera that anyone who took the COVID vaccine was no longer human and then "hinted" that killing something nonhuman wasn't really murder.

Canada announced contingency plans in case the U.S. came under authoritarian rule in the next election.

Autoworkers in the U.S. went on strike against all three major car manufacturers after executives raised their own pay by 40%, leaving the workers behind.

A woman arrested two years ago for protesting an oil pipeline in Minnesota was sentenced to five years in prison for sitting in a bamboo tower and briefly blocking construction equipment.

Friends to the End

I'd just entered Toby's score for A-L-A-K when "To Make You Feel My Love" started playing on Pandora. I stood, took a breath, and held out my hand. "May I have this dance?"

"Oh, Craig, you know I can't dance."

"No one's watching."

Toby looked at the Scrabble board and back up at me. Then he stood and took my hand. I pulled him close and we began slowly rocking back and forth as we turned in a circle. Basic high school slow dancing. His limp wasn't even noticeable.

I put my cheek against his. It felt like dancing with a stranger, but a stranger I liked and found attractive. I felt a spark. Then all too soon, the song ended and Toby sat back down. "Your turn."

B-U-N-N-Y. But at least the Y was on a double letter score.

A couple of turns later, while Toby was studying his tiles, my phone rang. Even with Jonah and Doug in my life, I still didn't get many texts, and neither of them called often. Maybe this was one of the new guys I'd messaged.

There was always room for another casual encounter that remained casual.

My instinct was to answer, but I knew how irritated I could feel when Toby abandoned me in the middle of our "quality time" to pay attention to someone else, and after the lovely dance, I didn't want to spoil anything.

"Go ahead and answer," Toby said. "I need to make a piss stop anyway."

"That's pit stop."

"I lisp more with all this extra testosterone in the air." He disappeared into the bathroom.

I picked up the phone and saw Jonah's name. "Hey," I said, swiping on the green phone icon. "What's up?"

"We goi dow!"

I wasn't sure I heard right. There was so much noise in the background and the connection wasn't great. "What?"

"Craig, we're…n…a terrible storm. We've los…n…engine. Probably…ail."

I leaped to my feet as if that would help me hear better.

"I wanted you to…in case I don't make…"

Oh my god.

"…that I sprayed black pai…all over…port manager's car in Okla..."

I gasped as if I'd been punched in the stomach. *That* was going to be Jonah's legacy?

I could hear screams in the background, and thumps. Maybe carry-on luggage being thrown about. A loud rushing noise.

"Craig—"

"Brace for impact." I could barely make out the captain's announcement.

The phone went dead.

"You all right?" Toby looked at me, frowning, still zipping up as he came out of the bathroom.

"Jonah's plane just crashed!"

Toby grabbed his wallet and keys from the end table. "Let's go," he said.

"Where?"

"The airport."

***

"Thanks for coming, Martin," I said after he and Toby embraced, Martin subconsciously standing on tip toe so Toby wouldn't need to bend over. He sometimes lifted his heels even when just speaking with Toby.

I found it adorable and oddly comforting.

"Of course."

Jonah's flight had crashed twenty miles out of Oklahoma City, not long after taking off, caught in a fast-developing thunderstorm. We waited with other family and friends in a large lounge to learn more details. All we knew so far was that some aboard the plane had survived…and some had not.

If Jonah had survived, why hadn't he called?

"Flight attendants have the best chance of anyone to survive," Toby said, putting a hand on my arm.

I couldn't stop thinking of Jonah's last words. What an epitaph.

Why had he called me and not his mother? They weren't estranged. Why not one of his long-time friends?

Why did he call *me*?

One wall of the lounge was made of windows, and the hot sun beat through them and into the room. Even with air conditioning, it was sweltering.

A single weather disaster was bad but not the end of the world. Just like a single drop of water wasn't the biggest deal. But Chinese water torture was a real thing. So were floods.

Every workable solution to the climate crisis involved eliminating capitalism. But did we need to wait until we adopted socialism to create meaningful action? What if that took fifty more years?

Martin handed me a bottle of unsweetened tea from a vending machine. I hadn't spoken to him about my diabetes but apparently Toby had.

The wait grew excruciating. I could see officials pulling aside this wife or that father and then leading them away, with neither good nor bad news obvious in anyone's expression. Finally, a man walked up to us. "Family of Jonah Borgonia?"

I jumped up and followed the man, Toby and Martin not far behind.

"Mr. Borgonia has suffered moderate injuries and been admitted to a hospital in Oklahoma City," the airline official told us once he'd led us into a small office.

Toby squeezed my left hand while Martin squeezed my right. I barely knew the man, and he was here for me.

I remembered a scene from *Starman*, where the alien tells Karen Allen what he finds most beautiful about the human species. "You're at your best when things are worst."

That movie was about a crash landing, too. I wondered if Jonah would want to watch.

We couldn't get any more details about Jonah's condition but did get contact information for the hospital, and then Toby, Martin, and I headed home. After weeks of considering the possibility, I decided to try to sleep while lying down again.

Toby slept in the middle.

***

"Doug, I need to do something you won't report me for but which you *should* report me for."

"Damn, Craig. I didn't even hear the news." He hugged me again. "Why didn't you call?"

"Bonding moment with Toby and Martin." I shook my head. "But I should have at least texted." I sighed. "Sometimes, I don't want you to be part of my family, but you absolutely are."

Doug blinked and held me once more.

"What do you want to do?"

I was conflating everything. I knew it. Maggie's death. The turmoil in all my relationships. Aging. Politics. Climate. Planes had been crashing during thunderstorms for a hundred years. This particular crash wasn't necessarily tied to climate breakdown.

But in my head, it was undeniable.

"How many drones do you have?"

"Five."

"And you said you had access to bombs? Or was that just to gauge my reaction?"

Doug blinked again. "I have access."

"Well, I looked it up online. There's an empty oil tanker docked in Tacoma. Let's see that it never carries oil again."

***

Before Jonah's last flight, we'd shared our reward for the tattoos. He'd invited two of his flight attendant friends over and asked them both to shoot onto his asshole and then take pictures of me licking off their cum.

Gay men were weird.

Praise Jesus.

One of the flight attendants wasn't even gay. But solidarity, I suppose, brought out the best in folks.

I spent a couple of hours last night selecting the best photos of me, him, our various body parts, and a multitude of our sexual interactions and then ordered ten fake passports, five for each of us. We could use them for more airplane role play when he recovered.

Would I be granted conjugal visits in prison?

I needed to take my mind off the impending attack on the ship in Tacoma and picked up some tacos from a street vendor on my way home from the drugstore. I could eat one if I took a few extra fiber capsules, and Toby loved hot taco sauce and could eat three.

"I went to the self-checkout line at the store," Toby said, "but there were no mirrors, so what was I supposed to do?"

It had been a long time since Toby had joked with me. He'd never been that great at it, but I appreciated the effort.

And while I didn't like hot taco sauce, I made sure to squirt a packet into my mouth before I rimmed Toby later. He expressed enough enthusiasm then for the both of us. I'd have to tell Martin to keep some packets on hand in their bedside table for special occasions.

Fire and Rain

An explosion at a fuel depot in Azerbaijan killed at least 170 people.

Hailstorms bashed in car windshields and damaged roofs across central Texas.

King County officials in Washington state asked residents to conserve water, saying the area was twenty-six inches short of its normal rain total for the year so far.

Trump was convicted of fraud in New York, all his business licenses canceled, and fined $250,000,000. In return, he did a photo op in South Carolina, buying a gun at the same chain where a white supremacist had purchased his before gunning down three black people. Under federal indictment, Trump wasn't legally allowed to purchase a gun.

Hundreds of looters ransacked dozens of stores across Philadelphia for two nights in a row.

A Republican representative from Colorado, caught groping her date in public, demanded that Congress reduce the annual salary of the Assistant Secretary of Defense Readiness to $1 because the official was transgender.

Over 82,000 Kaiser workers were preparing for a strike over safe staffing and other issues.

A huge spike in the deaths of gray whales was linked to decreasing Arctic ice.

Nowhere to Go but Down

I wasn't sure if I was an accessory or not. Even if Doug was the one pulling off the actual sinking, he was doing it at my request.

The trick, of course, was in getting the FBI to suspect someone other than Doug—or me—*and* for agents not to demand that Doug turn over someone else as the culprit. It would be great to pin it on some rightwing domestic terrorist. There were certainly lots of terrorist wannabes in the Pacific Northwest. But it turned out *we* were the bad guys.

Freedom fighters or rebel leaders?

I remembered the teenage Dutch girls who lured German soldiers to their deaths. Even Dutch children playing in the streets who ambushed and killed soldiers.

History was written by the victors.

I wondered if *anyone* would be in a position to write history fifty or a hundred years from now.

I carried Doug's phone as I wandered about Beacon Hill while he headed to Tacoma, hoping to provide at least a minimal alibi. The only way not to stress myself into a heart attack was to accept up front we'd be caught. It was worth making an attempt to cover our tracks, just in case, but not worth believing we'd succeed.

Afterward, Doug met me near light rail to pick up his phone, but we didn't talk about what he'd done. He headed on home and I did, too.

Toby had left a bag of boiled peanuts for me. He was spending the night at Martin's place so they could shout in the bedroom without disturbing me.

I rather liked hearing them shout.

***

"I uploaded the video," Doug said quietly, hugging me in his bedroom while our phones sat in a box in the living room, music playing to cover our whispers.

"You filmed yourself committing a crime?" He couldn't be serious. Why were we even bothering to whisper?

"I had five drones," he said softly. "Four of them carried bombs and one filmed the event. It's important for people to see action in action."

"But…but…"

"I'm sure the video can't be traced back to me. I've been forced to learn how to do these things."

People weren't usually good immediately with tasks that required a learning curve, and given the magnitude of the crime, we were probably doomed.

I'd just ordered the book *We're Doomed. Now What?* but felt too afraid to read it.

"Let's watch but only say things that sound like we're watching the news."

I took a deep breath and followed Doug to the sofa. I listened for the sound of an approaching SWAT team but heard nothing, and soon the image of an industrial area showed up on screen. There was Puget Sound, always lovely, tree-covered islands off to the west, and what looked like a bustling port to the east.

The drone's camera revealed five long inlets jutting in from the Sound and two small ones. The longest inlet seemed to be a river. I vaguely remembered a dispute with the Puyallup Tribe, who'd actually won their case in court, though I couldn't remember exactly what the dispute was about. A pipeline crossing their land?

The most obvious objects in the port weren't the ships but the towering cranes along the edges of the waterways. They had to be three or four hundred feet high, several painted blue, several more painted green, still others painted orange. Towers and towers of cranes that all looked as tall as forty-story buildings. None seemed to be in use but were almost certainly for loading and unloading container ships.

Three of those container ships were plainly visible. Two looked to have maybe three hundred containers each. Another must have carried at least eight hundred. And as tall as that ship was loaded with layer after layer of containers, the cranes still towered far above. A tugboat pulled on one of the ships, though I couldn't imagine how such a tiny boat could have any impact on a vessel hundreds of times its size.

Bombing an empty oil tanker would disrupt more than just the fossil fuel economy.

The port was larger than I'd imagined, certainly thousands of acres. I saw grain elevators and parking lots filled with imported cars, buildings that looked like factories. Railroad tracks carried cargo to and from ships. And there appeared to be an oil refinery right there on the property. I could see at least two dozen huge storage tanks.

I was just about to ask Doug a question when I saw the first explosion on the deck of a ship docked in one of the long waterways. It was followed a moment later by another explosion and then another. I didn't know what kind of bombs Doug had access to or what kind of payload a drone could carry, but dark clouds billowed from the vessel within seconds, flames peeking through. I could see additional explosions onboard as the fires ignited vulnerable engines or tanks or whatever flammable items were there.

I'd barely had the stamina to look up the location of the ship online but realized I needed to do far more research in the future if we were ever going to conduct another action. I had absolutely no clue what we were doing. I was a child throwing a rock into the darkness while camping and hoping it somehow hit the monster out in the woods.

I watched as people ran this way and that, some rushing off the ship, a few leaping into the water. There were more flames, more billowing smoke. I desperately hoped no one had been injured.

How did oil company CEOs look themselves in the mirror every day?

I watched as cars and trucks zoomed about. Flashing lights showed that a fire station at the port was responding.

Two helicopters zoomed into the picture from somewhere off to the east.

And then a fourth bomb exploded, on one of the largest oil tanks at the refinery. I remembered the blast in Beirut a few years earlier.

I saw my life behind bars. I saw myself being beaten in the showers. I saw guards paid off to stage my suicide.

But in the midst of the absolute dread and fear, I felt exuberance, too.

Taking out a single ship when there were thousands and thousands of oil tankers around the world was laughably trivial. But we'd done it. No matter what else happened, *we'd done it.*

A flash from one of the helicopters grew larger as an object approached the camera. Then the video ended.

I looked at Doug and he looked at me. Neither of us said a word. But I felt closer to him than I'd ever felt with any partner, however good the sex might have been, however rewarding the relationship might have been.

This was a passionate encounter. I suddenly understood what Toby wasn't getting from me.

And I felt deeply grateful he now had Martin in his life.

***

Jonah was due back in two days. When I spoke to him after eating my last soggy peanut, I didn't mention the ship sinking and he didn't, either. Perhaps he hadn't heard. And we had plenty of other things to discuss.

"It's not that I don't want to talk about the crash," he said from his hospital bed. "It's just different on TV. In a movie, you hear what the pilots are saying, see the instruments they're trying, you see what's happening with the air traffic controllers. You watch what the flight attendants are doing. You see what passengers are saying and doing. But when it's really happening, you're just shouting a few instructions and then…hanging on and crashing."

"We'll watch a shipwreck movie next time," I said. "I've got a DVD of *The Last Voyage*."

Jonah laughed but then groaned. "Ow, that hurt." He chuckled again. "Thanks."

"I suppose this'll put a kink in our sex lives for a while," I said wistfully.

"Kink. I like the sound of that."

Jonah was going to be okay. I could never tell him what he'd inspired me to do, of course, without jeopardizing his freedom. But I felt happy, regardless now how things might turn out for me.

I'd insisted Doug turn me over if agents grew too suspicious, tell them he'd only delayed reporting me because he wanted to be sure. There was an advantage to having lived a good life already. I didn't "need" to stay free.

"When you're up for it," I said, "you're going to spend another night with Toby, Martin, and me."

"And Doug, I assume. Are we moving to a five-bedroom mansion?"

"We won't all of us ever live together," I said. "Frankly, I don't think even where there are just two partners they should live under one roof. But once in a while, we'll all want to spend a night in the same bed. Kind of like touching base."

"I'm still pretty sore."

"Tell that to my ass."

"Okay. I'm interested again."

I chuckled a moment but then grew serious. "Thank you, Jonah," I said. "I mean it."

"For what?"

"For surviving."

***

Martin and I picked up Jonah from the airport. Toby had a medical appointment. Jonah had no luggage, so we walked directly to the parking lot. His left cheek was bruised, and there was a bandage covering part of his forehead. He had some internal injuries that were now stable enough for him to be ambulatory. His left arm was in a cast.

He hadn't broken it during the crash. A passenger pushing past him as Jonah guided others onto the slide knocked him out of the plane with a carry-on and he missed the slide altogether.

Jonah kissed us both, though his kiss with Martin was more tentative.

"How's our up and coming star?" I asked.

Jonah frowned. "I already told you I'm getting a tattoo of a dragon on my dick?"

Martin coughed, choking maybe on his spit.

"Um, no." But good to know. "I assume you'll be on a future episode of *Mayday*?"

He instinctively looked at his cast. "I'll have some choice things to say about evacuation procedures *and* greenhouse gases that'll only make them more common in the coming years."

Certain sponsors had a way of editing out comments like those, but there was no point mentioning that today.

When we arrived at Jonah's apartment, we all walked up together. I could see the relief on Jonah's face once he was back in a familiar space. "I'm going to leave you two here to get better acquainted," I said. "I'll catch the bus home."

Martin looked from Jonah to me and back to Jonah. "This is all so weird," he said. "But I kind of like it."

Jonah smiled. "You've become a flight attendant yourself, haven't you, Craig? Guiding us all through the turbulence."

I nudged Martin. "Ask him what he likes to do on the loveseat."

"I doubt I'll need many guesses."

Jonah feigned outrage but could only put one hand on his hip. "Are you saying I'm *predictable*?"

I left them then to do something unpredictable and headed home. Just for the hell of it, I stopped at Safeway first and bought some yellow carnations. Yellow was Toby's favorite color.

When he came home half an hour after me, he was carrying a small bouquet of purple Gerbera daisies. He handed them to me with a shrug. "I felt we needed something gay in the house."

Then I blew him while he reached over me to make himself a sandwich for lunch.

I think I had the better condiment squeeze bottle.

Terrorism

Torrential rains in Greece washed cars and buses into the sea. Then the rains moved east and pummeled Turkey and Bulgaria, one of the worst floods in European history.

Heavy flooding in Brazil killed dozens.

Hong Kong experienced its heaviest rainfall since records began 139 years ago.

A former right-wing presidential candidate suggested that if the left won the next election, it would be the last election decided with ballots instead of bullets.

Hurricane Lee grew from a Category 1 storm to a Category 5 in less than twenty-four hours.

For the first time since humans began keeping records, a Category 5 storm formed in each of the seven tropical oceans around the world during the same year.

Over 11,000 people drowned after two dams burst during heavy rains in Libya.

After the hottest June on record, the hottest July, and the hottest August, the Earth had just experienced the warmest summer on record for the northern hemisphere and the warmest winter on record for the southern hemisphere.

Young people banded together to sue thirty-two governments in the European Court of Human Rights for their failure to address climate change.

After a second round of devastating floods in the course of a few weeks, the Greek government declared that adapting to climate change was now a national priority.

Then it increased the work week to 78 hours over six days and eliminated work breaks so that its citizens would be too exhausted to protest or fight for anything at all.

A Day at the Park

"It's not too late to join a book club and lead a slower paced life." Doug looked at me, trying to keep his expression blank.

"Oh, I think it is." I forced a smile I didn't really feel.

"You sure you want to do another action already?"

"The FBI may be on their way to arrest us this very minute for Tacoma." Earlier that morning, I'd watched a news clip of activists somewhere in Europe—was it Germany?—who'd been pummeled with pressurized spray from water cannons, so much force striking them that two of the activists ended up with kidney damage.

"I don't have any more drones," Doug said, "and we can't be seen buying them again anytime soon."

Wouldn't it be nice, I thought, if one of Doug's FBI contacts already knew Doug and I were the ones responsible and was consciously protecting us? If there was ever a time when succeeding took a village, it was now.

Doug and I stuffed flyers into our backpacks and drove to Georgetown. We parked around the corner from the dental office located in the former Georgetown City Hall. The building was so close to Boeing Field that it had a blinking light on top to warn planes not to fly too low.

We weren't distributing anything inflammatory today, no calls for violence or attacks on fossil fuel infrastructure, just a full sheet of copy paper divided into quarters. Three of the sections had simple, clear photos—a burned church, a body floating face down in a flooded city, and a forlorn, starving child with protruding ribs. The final section featured three requests:

Don't Let Rich People Bake the Planet

Act Because Acting Matters

Don't Leave the Solution Up to Others

Of course, any solution short of a full transition away from fossil fuels was doomed to failure, including our action today. I had to see these tiny efforts as a single nail in a hundred-story building. One nail or screw or light switch cover wasn't going to make or break a building, but for that building to function properly and finally be opened to the public, it was going to take every single component added in the right spot at the right time.

I wanted to be the best screw I could be.

I kind of wished I was doing this action today with Jonah. Doug could do something more daring. But Jonah was busy working with union leaders while on sick leave, doing what he could to push for a better contract. There were plenty of other problems in the world to address. And labor issues were how we'd met in the first place.

Doug and I walked along Ellis, shoving flyers into mailboxes. Technically, that was against the law. We were supposed to stick them in door cracks or roll them up and balance them between doorknobs and door frames. But they kept falling to the ground and getting blown away. It was hot today, and the wind was drying my skin. It seemed to dry more and more easily as I grew older.

After the first block, we took a side street and then headed back up on Flora. I pulled out some lotion.

"You carry lotion in your fanny pack?" Doug asked.

I shrugged. "I don't like finding myself in a public restroom with a promising dick and no way to accommodate it."

I dabbed some on my face and then my hands before offering the tiny bottle to Doug. I let him massage the lotion into my forehead and cheeks while I massaged the dabs he dotted about his face into his skin.

"You can turn the most mundane acts into…"

"Yes?"

"I was going to say 'sexual thrills' but that's not quite true. It's more like…"

"Intimacy?"

Doug smiled.

After we finished stuffing mailboxes on Flora, we moved over to Carleton and back down again. Then over to Corson and up. We planned to go along the full length of all these streets, up and down each block, inching downward like a crab, all the way to Marginal Way. This was going to take a few more hours.

“Let’s stop at Oxbow Park for a water break.”

We sat on a bench between the giant cowboy hat and the two giant cowboy boots. I remembered watching the show *Land of the Giants* as a child.

“Are we stochastic terrorists?” I asked.

“Because we’re hoping to inspire people to take action on their own?”

“I saw a report this morning about someone shooting out windshields at a car dealership in Texas.”

“But no message attached?”

I shook my head.

“I prefer the term ‘stochastic activism.’” Doug took another sip of water.

Terminology didn’t change facts, of course, any more than greenwashing ads by fossil fuel companies reduced emissions.

I supposed everyone needed a little delusion in their life. If I could pretend what we were doing mattered, it wasn’t that different from a religious person who believed they were heading to heaven one day. What more could we ask of our beliefs than they help us get through difficult lives?

“I think—”

Suddenly, the ground shook so violently that I stumbled and sat back down on the bench to keep from falling. Were we having an earthquake? It had been over twenty years since the last big one, not long before Toby and I got together.

Windows rattled in the buildings near us. Car alarms started blaring. A tremendous roar filled the air.

The ground stopped shaking, but the roar continued.

Doug and I both jumped up and looked toward the sound. Huge, dark clouds were billowing over toward the freeway. Had a plane crashed short of the runway? That was the last thing Jonah needed to hear about.

"A train must have derailed!" Doug shouted. Folks were coming out of their homes and apartments and turning toward the cataclysm.

I remembered now that railroad tracks passed between Boeing Field and the freeway, and given the color of the smoke, oil seemed to be the cargo. I felt relief that it wasn't a plane and then guilt for feeling relief.

And then wondered if Doug had placed a bomb on the tracks without telling me.

For better or for worse, he'd have wanted me to know.

I wanted to see for myself, be a citizen journalist, maybe take a few photos with my phone and use them to illustrate one of the most common dangers from oil transport.

Who could forget the horrors in Mégantic?

"That smoke's toxic," Doug said. "We'd better head out."

"Your car's there." I pointed toward the black clouds.

"Too late to worry about that now." He motioned, and we started walking quickly toward Marginal Way but still stuffing mailboxes as we went. We hadn't covered half a block, though, before we heard half a dozen more explosions.

Three cars zoomed past, heading away from the derailment. Then two more. And another three. The roar of the flames was deafening, even from this distance. And the screams.

Why were people screaming?

"Craig," Doug said, his voice so subdued I could barely hear him over the other sounds, "*Georgetown's* on fire."

We could see more than black smoke now. Flames spreading north and south over at least three or four blocks shot up above the buildings between us and the disaster. We heard car horns blaring, sirens, trucks rushing by a street over. And more screams.

People were running toward us from the fire.

We were in the middle of a major city. We weren't going to burn down. This wasn't the French Quarter of New Orleans in 1788.

I could hear crackling in addition to everything else. I could smell the fire approaching. The wind had picked up.

Doug tore off his backpack and threw it on the ground, helping me pull mine off a moment later. We joined throngs of other pedestrians and started running.

I wanted to call Toby, call Jonah. How had he managed to call me as his plane went down? I was suddenly touched as I realized the effort that must have taken.

Doug pulled on my arm, urging me to move faster. I was too old and fat for this. I remembered that most of the dead in Lahaina had been elderly.

"Don't wait for me, Doug." I waved him on. He shook his head and kept pulling. A young boy on a bicycle rode past, followed by a teen on a skateboard. A thirty-something black man jogged by as if in no big hurry.

But I had to stop for a second and catch my breath. When I turned to look behind us, I saw that the buildings just past the park were burning. As I watched, the cowboy hat caught fire.

Those flames were moving *fast*. The hot, dry weather and thousands of gallons of oil were hardly things to dampen them.

Doug grabbed me again and started off. I followed as quickly as I could. Dying of a heart attack was a thousand times better than burning to death. I could push myself to the limit. We ran another block, and another.

A heavyset Latina half walked, half ran, lagging even farther behind than a heavy white woman who also wasn't doing so well. Two black teenage girls sprinted past and kept going.

A black teenage boy stopped to help the Latina.

My lungs burned, my side hurt. My leg muscles were on the verge of cramping. I remembered Toby's frustration with my charley horses. Doug didn't say anything, not wasting his energy talking. Others running past had stopped screaming, too focused on their own efforts now. No more cars passed.

Anyone able to drive out had already jumped in their cars and escaped.

I remembered the last images I'd seen of Maggie. The last sounds.

I could hear the fire behind us, the pounding of feet on the pavement, and the huffing and gasping of people running for their lives. If there were any other sounds, I didn't register them.

Other than the blood throbbing in my head. I was going to have a stroke. That might be worse than burning to death. My legs were about to give out. But I kept running.

When was it time to just give up?

Doug and I finally reached Marginal Way. Traffic was still crazy here, some people slowing to look over toward the freeway and others trying to get past to safety. Here there was all kinds of noise, buses and trucks and vans, honking and cursing, brakes squealing.

I turned to look back. The flames couldn't be two blocks away. Half the neighborhood was already gone. All in the space of a few minutes.

"We can't stop." Doug pulled me across the street, right through the traffic.

I had no ATP left. My legs had nothing to work with. I couldn't take another step.

I hoped Doug and Jonah and Toby and Martin would still work on their foursome without me.

Doug gave me thirty seconds to catch my breath, watching the smoke and flames racing toward us. This part of Georgetown was industrial, and we couldn't go any farther on Corson. We had to turn south until we hit Carleton again. A block farther, and we turned onto Myrtle. And from there, it was a race to the river.

The dirty Duwamish had never looked lovelier.

I collapsed on the riverbank. Dozens of other people splashed out into the water. I really only registered two of them. A white mother stood waist deep in the water, clutching her five-year-old daughter, the child's face buried in her mother's shoulder, the mother's face a picture of pure despair.

I wondered if she had another child.

The screams I could hear in the distance now weren't screams of fear. They were screams of agony.

Debris

Eight inches of rain fell in New York City in just a few hours, flooding much of the city and forcing inundated subway stations in Brooklyn to close.

A man with a hammer hit two elderly people in the head at the Beacon Hill light rail station in Seattle. A man was shot and killed on the bus in White Center.

Democratic members of Congress reported receiving over 9000 death threats since the beginning of the year.

At least twenty-nine people died as heavy rains swept away homes in Guatemala.

Several climate advocates, not activists, were arrested in Vietnam.

Flash flooding in India washed away eleven bridges after a dam holding back a glacial lake burst during heavy rains.

The water temperature in Lake Tefé in Brazil reached 102 degrees F. At least 125 river dolphins overheated and died.

News video showed a mile-long line of fire approaching Villa Carlos Paz, a city of 56,000, in Argentina. Over 2700 wildfires broke out across the Amazon in a two-week period.

For the first time ever recorded, sea ice that melted during the summer along parts of Antarctica's coast did not reform during the winter, leaving large stretches of the coastline bare.

A fire at a car park at Luton airport in London left over 1400 cars burned out shells.

A Catholic priest in the U.S. called for the assassination of the pope for being too soft on LGBTQ issues.

Eight people were killed and dozens injured in a 168-car pileup in Louisiana as smoke from marsh fires combined with a dense fog to create a "superfog" event.

The EU began implementing a Europe-wide carbon tax on imported goods including cement, steel, fertilizer, and electricity.

A Danish company canceled plans to build two wind farms off the coast of New Jersey, citing inflation and high interest rates.

Golden, Silver, and Bronze Men

The fire missed the South Seattle College campus and stopped at Boeing Field. It had taken out a dozen or so businesses and over 1200 homes and apartments across thirty blocks. Seventeen people had been killed, the same as the number of students killed in the latest school shooting.

Doug's car was a mass of charred metal. The insurance company seemed to be in no hurry to pay him.

Even folks attuned to the realities of poverty were often surprised at the difficulty of *always* using public transit to get around rather than only when it was convenient. But Doug was nothing if not adaptive. Over the next couple of weeks, we traveled by bus and light rail to deliver more flyers. We simply weren't up to anything more demanding yet.

Since Doug's "job" was to be an informer, he didn't really need to commute to and from work, and Martin offered to take him to the grocery if he needed to buy anything heavy.

Jonah was still a few weeks away from having his cast removed, making the most of his time to work with his union. Doug loaned him some DVDs to brush up on labor history. *Matawan*, *Made in Dagenham*, *Salt of the Earth*, and *Pride*.

But we were all taking more time to relax. Neither Doug nor I had been questioned yet about the incident in Tacoma. All the news these days was on climate change and train safety. Still, I occasionally found myself humming the Sword of Damocles song from *Rocky Horror*.

Last Friday, all five of us had dressed as characters from the movie while we watched it at midnight at our place. We used *Real Change* newspapers to shield us from the water pistols.

And now we were spending Sunday night together again.

"Think of all the moral outrage over our 'lifestyle' but none for the climate 'abominations' wiping out jobs and homes and lives." Doug shook his head. "These folks are worried about two guys fucking. Or three. Or four or five. *That's* beyond the pale."

"There's no end to the story, is there?" I asked. "No climax and then things get back to normal." I felt like singing "The Neverending Story." If only I had a cute dragon to ride.

Well, there was Jonah.

He shrugged. "We can take breaks once in a while. Even soldiers go on leave. We're of no use if we burn out."

Burn out. The term took on an added meaning during climate change.

"I was burning out before I met you guys," I said. "You can be crushed just by everyday life. You guys saved me."

I thought about food banks, and the Black Panthers, and other efforts at mutual aid. Activism was mutual aid, too. When we did it well, we provided hope and meaning, both essential for survival.

Toby and Martin soon returned from the basement, and we all began settling in to watch a movie. *Men to Kiss*, a German comedy.

We needed a new Susan Harris to develop a comedy about five partnered men sharing a life together.

Casual sex didn't mean that love was absent…or present, for that matter. But when the love was there, too, casual sex was like a sweet "good morning" delivered with a cup of hot coffee.

Tomorrow, we had an appointment to tour another Craftsman a few doors down, two stories and with four bedrooms. If we liked it, and the price seemed right, we might all go in together on the purchase so that two of us could live in one residence—probably Toby and Martin—and the rest of us in the other. And still be close enough to visit and play and chill regularly.

Chill. That word sure took on an added meaning during global warming, too.

It felt foolish to be purchasing a home when one or more of us might be arrested at any moment, but failing to plan for the future we wanted felt even more foolish.

The new house had a large basement. We could start storing cans of oil, storing drones, build up slowly over a few months and then plan something big again. Maybe only a few big events each year and then try to live and love the rest of the time. Not many cycles left with the latest report stating that rapid melting of West Antarctica's ice shelves was now irreversible. But perhaps some other tipping points could still be averted.

I was already thinking about what our next action might be. We could even head down to Portland to do it.

“I don’t want to sit on the floor,” Jonah said. There was only room for four of us on the sofa, and the easy chair was too far away.

I patted my lap, and he wasted no time wriggling onto me. I wrapped my arms around him, Toby dimmed the lights, Doug reached over to put his hand on Jonah’s thigh, and then Martin pressed Play.

Books by Johnny Townsend

Thanks for reading! If you enjoyed this book, could you please take a few minutes to write a review online? Reviews are helpful both to me as an author and to other readers, so we'd all sincerely appreciate your writing one! And if you did enjoy the book, here are some others I've written you might want to look up:

Mormon Underwear

A Gay Mormon Missionary in Pompeii

The Golem of Rabbi Loew

Marginal Mormons

Sexual Solidarity

The Mysterious Madness of Mormons

Going-Out-Of-Religion Sale

Escape from Zion

Gayrabian Nights

Invasion of the Spirit Snatchers

Sins of the Saints

Mormon Misfits

Gay Gaslighting

Out of the Missionary's Closet

A Mormon Motive for Murder

Breaking the Promise of the Promised Land

Mormon Misfits

I Will, Through the Veil

Am I My Planet's Keeper?

Have Your Cum and Eat It, Too

Strangers with Benefits

Constructing Equity

Wake Up and Smell the Missionaries

Racism by Proxy

Orgy at the STD Clinic

Please Evacuate

Recommended Daily Humanity

The Camper Killings

Repent! The End of Capitalism is Nigh!

Kinky Quilts: Patchwork Designs for Gay Men

An Eternity of Mirrors: Best Short Stories of Johnny Townsend

Inferno in the French Quarter: The UpStairs Lounge Fire

Latter-Gay Saints: An Anthology of Gay Mormon Fiction (co-editor)

Available from your favorite online or neighborhood bookstore.

Wondering what some of those other books are about? Read on!

Gayrabian Nights

Gayrabian Nights is a twist on the well-known classic, *1001 Arabian Nights*, in which Scheherazade, under the threat of death if she ceases to captivate King Shahryar's attention, enchants him through a series of mysterious, adventurous, and romantic tales.

In this variation, a male escort, invited to the hotel room of a closeted, homophobic Mormon senator, learns that the man is poised to vote on a piece of anti-gay legislation the following morning. To prevent him from sleeping, so that the exhausted senator will miss casting his vote on the Senate floor, the escort entertains him with stories of homophobia, celibacy, mixed orientation marriages, reparative therapy, coming out, first love, gay marriage, and long-term successful gay relationships.

The escort crafts the stories to give the senator a crash course in gay culture and sensibilities, hoping to bring the man closer to accepting his own sexual orientation.

Inferno in the French Quarter: The UpStairs Lounge Fire

On Gay Pride Day in 1973, someone set the entrance to a French Quarter gay bar on fire. In the terrible inferno that followed, thirty-two people lost their lives, including a third of the local congregation of the Metropolitan Community Church, their pastor burning to death halfway out a second-story window as he tried to claw his way to freedom.

A mother who'd gone to the bar with her two gay sons died alongside them. A man who'd helped his friend escape first was found dead near the fire escape.

Two children waited outside a movie theater across town for a father and "uncle" who would never pick them up. During this era of rampant homophobia, several families refused to claim the bodies, and many churches refused to bury the dead.

Author Johnny Townsend pored through old records and tracked down survivors of the fire as well as relatives and friends of those killed to compile this fascinating account of a forgotten moment in gay history.

This second edition on the 50th anniversary of the fire includes additional research and information not available previously.

Orgy at the STD Clinic

Todd Tillotson is struggling to move on after his husband is killed in a hit and run attack a year earlier during a Black Lives Matter protest in Seattle.

In this novel set entirely on public transportation, we watch as Todd, isolated throughout the pandemic, battles desperation in his attempt to safely reconnect with the world.

Will he find love again, even casual friendship, or will he simply end up another crazy old man on the bus?

Things don't look good until a man whose face he can't even see sits down beside him despite the raging variants.

And asks him a question that will change his life.

Please Evacuate

A gay, partygoing New Yorker unconcerned about the future or the unsustainability of capitalism is hit by a truck and thrust into a straight man's body half a continent away. As Hunter tries to figure out what's happening, he's caught up in another disaster, a wildfire sweeping through a Colorado community, the flames overtaking him and several schoolchildren as they flee.

When he awakens, Hunter finds himself in the body of yet another man, this time in northern Italy, a former missionary about to marry a young Mormon woman. Still piecing together this new reality, and beginning to embrace his latest identity, Hunter fights for his life in a devastating flash flood along with his wife *and* his new husband.

He's an aging worker in drought-stricken Texas, a nurse at an assisted living facility in the direct path of a hurricane, an advocate for the unhoused during a freak Seattle blizzard.

We watch as Hunter is plunged into life after life, finally recognizing the futility of only looking out for #1 and understanding the part he must play in addressing the global climate crisis…if he ever gets another chance.

The Camper Killings

When a homeless man is found murdered a few blocks from Morgan Beylerian's house in south Seattle, everyone seems to consider the body just so much additional trash to be cleared from the neighborhood. But Morgan liked the guy. They used to chat when Morgan brought Nick groceries once a week.

And the brutal way the man was killed reminds Morgan of their shared Mormon heritage, back when the faithful agreed to have their throats slit if they ever revealed temple secrets.

Did Nick's former wife take action when her ex-husband refused to grant a temple divorce? Did his murder have something to do with the public accusations that brought an end to his promising career?

Morgan does his best to investigate when no one else seems to care, but it isn't easy as a man living paycheck to paycheck himself, only able to pursue his investigation via public transit.

As he continues his search for the killer, Morgan's friends withdraw and his husband threatens to leave. When another homeless man is killed and Morgan is accused of the crime, things look even bleaker.

But his troubles aren't over yet.

Will Morgan find the killer before the killer finds him?

Kinky Quilts

Since patchwork quilts are usually displayed in bedrooms where couples engage in sex, why are there so few quilt designs for folks who want a bit of sexual energy in these intimate spaces?

The original designs in this volume range from simple to intermediate, and with over 250 to choose from, even beginner quilters will find patterns tempting enough to get started.

What Readers Have Said

Townsend's stories are "a gay *Portnoy's Complaint* of Mormonism. Salacious, sweet, sad, insightful, insulting, religiously ethnic, quirky-faithful, and funny."

D. Michael Quinn, author of *The Mormon Hierarchy: Origins of Power*

"Told from a believably conversational first-person perspective, [*A Gay Mormon Missionary in Pompeii*'s] novelistic focus on Anderson's journey to thoughtful self-acceptance allows for greater character development than often seen in short stories, which makes this well-paced work rich and satisfying, and one of Townsend's strongest. An extremely important contribution to the field of Mormon fiction." Named to Kirkus Reviews' Best of 2011.

Kirkus Reviews

"The thirteen stories in *Mormon Underwear* capture this struggle [between Mormonism and homosexuality] with humor, sadness, insight, and sometimes shocking details….*Mormon Underwear* provides compelling stories, literally from the inside-out."

Niki D'Andrea, *Phoenix New Times*

"Townsend's lively writing style and engaging characters [in *Zombies for Jesus*] make for stories which force us to wake up, smell the (prohibited) coffee, and review our attitudes with regard to reading dogma so doggedly. These are tales which revel in the individual tics and quirks which make us human, Mormon or not, gay or not…"

A.J. Kirby, *The Short Review*

"The Rift," from *A Gay Mormon Missionary in Pompeii*, is a "fascinating tale of an untenable situation…a *tour de force*."

David Lenson, editor, *The Massachusetts Review*

"Pronouncing the Apostrophe," from *The Golem of Rabbi Loew*, is "quiet and revealing, an intriguing tale…"

Sima Rabinowitz, Literary Magazine Review, *NewPages.com*

The Circumcision of God is "a collection of short stories that consider the imperfect, silenced majority of Mormons, who may in fact be [the Church's] best hope….[The book leaves] readers regretting the church's willingness to marginalize those who best exemplify its ideals: those who love fiercely despite all obstacles, who brave challenges at great personal risk and who always choose the hard, higher road."

Kirkus Reviews

In *Mormon Fairy Tales*, Johnny Townsend displays "both a wicked sense of irony and a deep well of compassion."

Kel Munger, *Sacramento News and Review*

Zombies for Jesus is "eerie, erotic, and magical."

Publishers Weekly

"While [Townsend's] many touching vignettes draw deeply from Mormon mythology, history, spirituality and culture, [*Mormon Fairy Tales*] is neither a gaudy act of proselytism nor angry protest literature from an ex-believer. Like all good fiction, his stories are simply about the joys, the hopes and the sorrows of people."

Kirkus Reviews

"In *Inferno in the French Quarter* author Johnny Townsend restores this tragic event [the UpStairs Lounge fire] to its proper place in LGBT history and reminds us that the victims of the blaze were not just 'statistics,' but real people with real lives, families, and friends."

Jesse Monteagudo, *The Bilerico Project*

In *Inferno in the French Quarter*, "Townsend's heart-rending descriptions of the victims…seem to [make them] come alive once more."

Kit Van Cleave, *OutSmart Magazine*

"While [*Inferno in the French Quarter*] is a non-fiction work, the author is a skilled fiction [writer], so he manages to respect the realism of the story, while at the same time recreating their lives and voices. It's probably thanks to the [author's] skills that this piece of non-fiction goes well beyond a simple recording of events."

Elisa Rolle, *Rainbow Awards*

Marginal Mormons is "an irreverent, honest look at life outside the mainstream Mormon Church….Throughout his musings on sin and forgiveness, Townsend beautifully demonstrates his characters' internal, perhaps irreconcilable struggles….Rather than anger and disdain, he offers an honest portrayal of people searching for meaning and community in their lives, regardless of their life choices or secrets." Named to Kirkus Reviews' Best of 2012.

Kirkus Reviews

The stories in *The Mormon Victorian Society* "register the new openness and confidence of gay life in the age of same-sex marriage….What hasn't changed is Townsend's wry, conversational prose, his subtle evocations of character and social dynamics, and his deadpan humor. His warm empathy still glows in this intimate yet clear-eyed engagement with Mormon theology and folkways. Funny, shrewd and finely wrought dissections of the awkward contradictions—and surprising harmonies—between conscience and desire." Named to Kirkus Reviews' Best of 2013.

Kirkus Reviews

"This collection of short stories [*The Mormon Victorian Society*] featuring gay Mormon characters slammed [me] in the face from the first page, wrestled my heart and mind to the floor, and left me panting and wanting more by the end. Johnny Townsend has created so many memorable characters in such few pages. I went weeks thinking about this book. It truly touched me."

Tom Webb, *A Bear on Books*

Dragons of the Book of Mormon is an "entertaining collection....Townsend's prose is sharp, clear, and easy to read, and his characters are well rendered..."

Publishers Weekly

"The pre-eminent documenter of alternative Mormon lifestyles...Townsend has a deep understanding of his characters, and his limpid prose, dry humor and well-grounded (occasionally magical) realism make their spiritual conundrums both compelling and entertaining. [*Dragons of the Book of Mormon* is] [a]nother of Townsend's critical but affectionate and absorbing tours of Mormon discontent." Named to Kirkus Reviews' Best of 2014.

Kirkus Reviews

In *Gayrabian Nights*, "Townsend's prose is always limpid and evocative, and...he finds real drama and emotional depth in the most ordinary of lives."

Kirkus Reviews

Gayrabian Nights is a "complex revelation of how seriously soul damaging the denial of the true self can be."

Ryan Rhodes, author of *Free Electricity*

Gayrabian Nights "was easily the most original book I've read all year. Funny, touching, topical, and thoroughly enjoyable."

Rainbow Awards

Lying for the Lord is "one of the most gripping books that I've picked up for quite a while. I love the author's writing style, alternately cynical, humorous, biting, scathing, poignant, and touching.... This is the third book of his that I've read, and all are equally engaging. These are stories that need to be told, and the author does it in just the right way."

Heidi Alsop, *Ex-Mormon Foundation Board Member*

In *Lying for the Lord*, Townsend "gets under the skin of his characters to reveal their complexity and conflicts....shrewd, evocative [and] wryly humorous."

Kirkus Reviews

In *Missionaries Make the Best Companions*, "the author treats the clash between religious dogma and liberal humanism with vivid realism, sly humor, and subtle feeling as his characters try to figure out their true missions in life. Another of Townsend's rich dissections of Mormon failures and uncertainties..." Named to Kirkus Reviews' Best of 2015.

Kirkus Reviews

In *Invasion of the Spirit Snatchers*, "Townsend, a confident and practiced storyteller, skewers the hypocrisies and eccentricities of his characters with precision and affection. The outlandish framing narrative is the most consistent source of shock and humor, but the stories do much to ground the reader in the world—or former world—of the characters....A funny, charming tale about a group of Mormons facing the end of the world."

Kirkus Reviews

"Townsend's collection [*The Washing of Brains*] once again displays his limpid, naturalistic prose, skillful narrative chops, and his subtle insights into psychology...Well-crafted dispatches on the clash between religion and self-fulfillment..."

Kirkus Reviews

"While the author is generally at his best when working as a satirist, there are some fine, understated touches in these tales [*The Last Days Linger*] that will likely affect readers in subtle ways....readers should come away impressed by the deep empathy he shows for all his characters—even the homophobic ones."

Kirkus Reviews

"Written in a conversational style that often uses stories and personal anecdotes to reveal larger truths, this immensely approachable book [*Racism by Proxy*] skillfully serves its intended audience of White readers grappling with complex questions regarding race, history, and identity. The author's frequent references to the Church of Jesus Christ of Latter-day Saints may be too niche for readers unfamiliar with its idiosyncrasies, but Townsend generally strikes a perfect balance of humor, introspection, and reasoned arguments that will engage even skeptical readers."

Kirkus Reviews

Orgy at the STD Clinic portrays "an all-too real scenario that Townsend skewers to wincingly accurate proportions...[with]

instant classic moments courtesy of his punchy, sassy, sexy lead character…"

Jim Piechota, *Bay Area Reporter*

Orgy at the STD Clinic is "…a triumph of humane sensibility. A richly textured saga that brilliantly captures the fraying social fabric of contemporary life." Named to Kirkus Reviews' Best Indie Books of 2022.

Kirkus Reviews

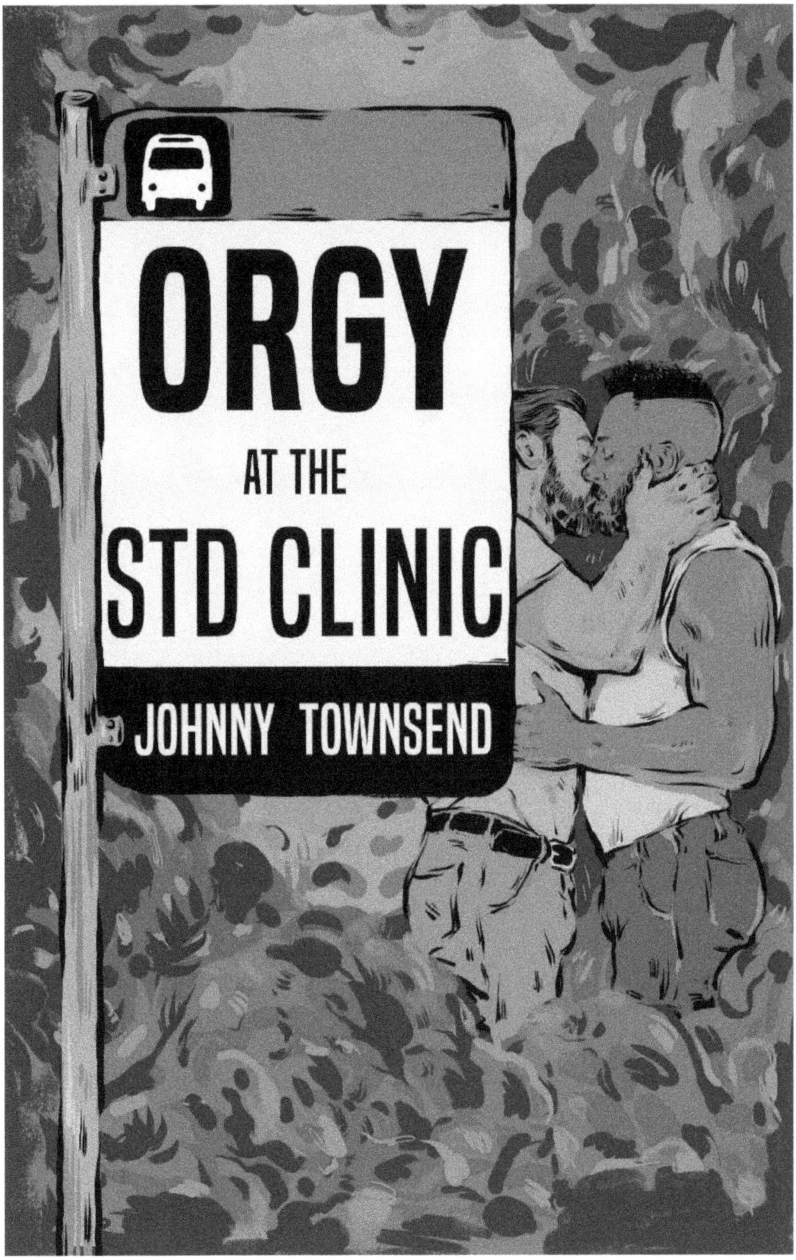
ORGY
AT THE
STD CLINIC
JOHNNY TOWNSEND

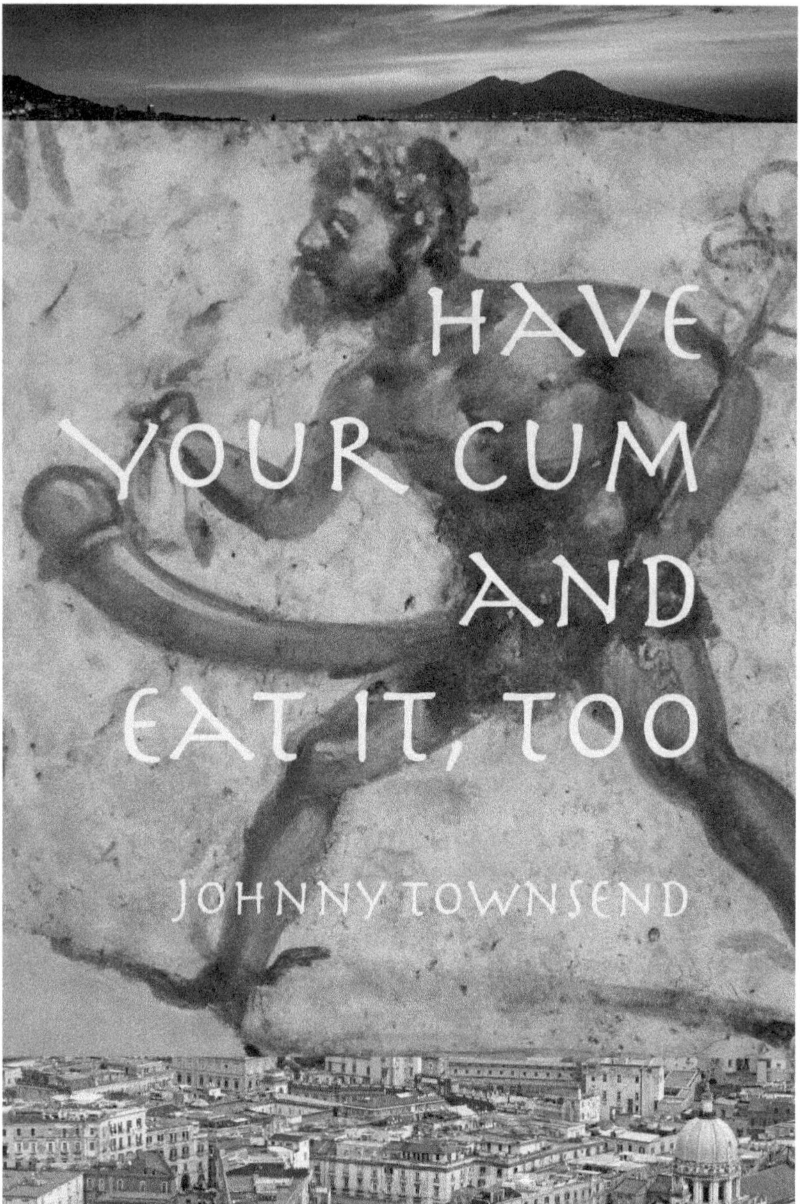
HAVE
YOUR CUM
AND
EAT IT, TOO
JOHNNY TOWNSEND

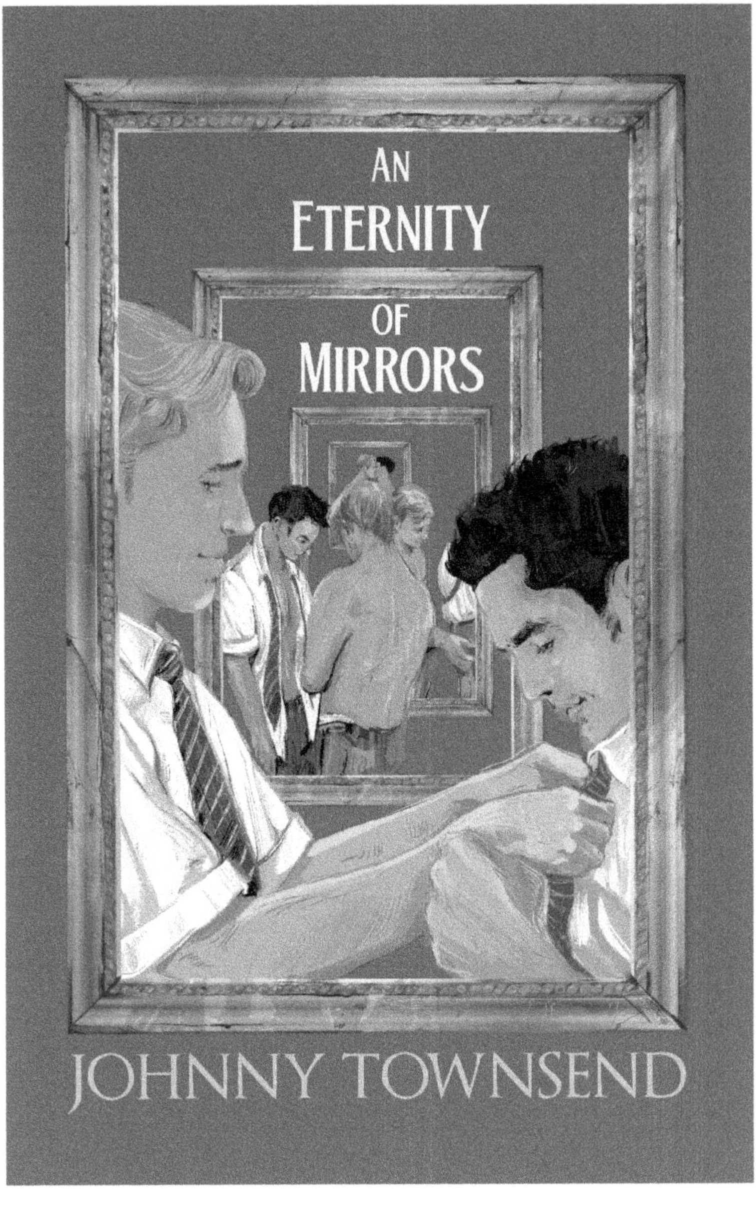
AN
ETERNITY
OF
MIRRORS
JOHNNY TOWNSEND

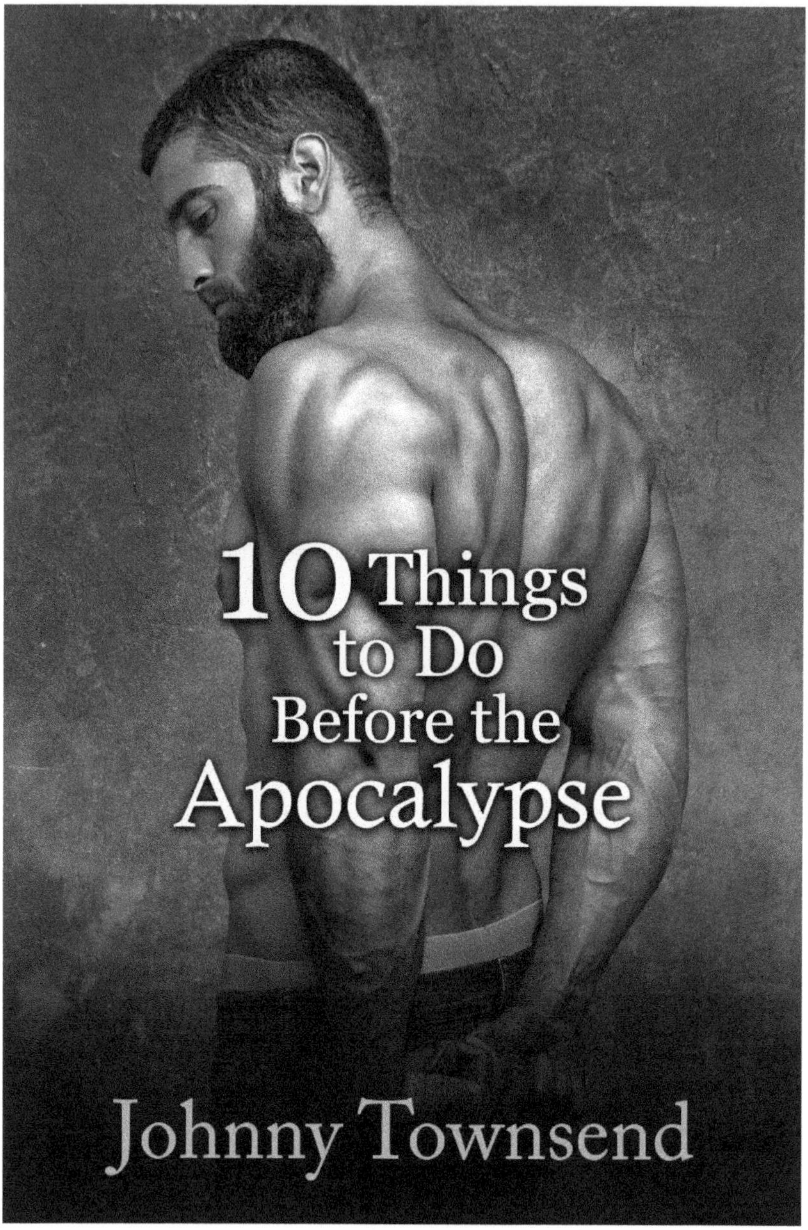
10 Things
to Do
Before the
Apocalypse
Johnny Townsend

Prepararsi
all'impatto
JOHNNY TOWNSEND

Milton Keynes UK
Ingram Content Group UK Ltd.
UKHW040854301024
450479UK00001B/27